JILL TRESEDER was born
childhood in sight of the s
Cornwall and West Wales. S
Devon overlooking the River

After graduating from Bri _____ German, Jill
followed careers in social work, management development and
social research, obtaining a PhD from the School of Management at the University of Bath along the way.

Since 2006 she has focused on writing fiction.

ALSO BY JILL TRESEDER

A Place of Safety
Becoming Fran
The Hatmaker's Secret

THE SATURDAY LETTERS

JILL TRESEDER

Sara

best reading Sis

lots of love

Jill xx

x November 2017

SilverWood

Originally published in 2017 as an ebook by sBooks
an imprint of SilverWood Books Ltd

This paperback edition published by SilverWood Books 2017

SilverWood Books Ltd
14 Small Street, Bristol, BS1 1DE, United Kingdom
www.silverwoodbooks.co.uk

ISBN 978-1-78132-739-5 (paperback)
ISBN 978-1-78132-714-2 (sBooks ebook)

British Library Cataloguing in Publication Data
A CIP catalogue record for this book is available from the British Library

Page design and typesetting by SilverWood Books
Printed on responsibly sourced paper

Author's Note

Henrietta, the letter writer, was brought up in Bermuda by her mother and grandmother who came from Barbados. They spoke Bajan (pronounced Bājan with a long 'a', as in Bar*bājan*), a language originally developed amongst slaves on the sugar plantations as a covert means of communication. It has survived and evolved and is widely used on the island today, alongside Standard English, especially in informal domestic and social settings.

I have aimed to convey the flavour of the language while making it understandable to the English reader.

It will be useful to know the following terms:

Cheese-on-bread – an exclamation of surprise or irritation with the English equivalents 'My word!' or 'Oh, bother!'
Pickney – a word adopted from Jamaica meaning a small child.
Jipsy – nosey.
Pompasetting – showing off.
Duppies – dead people; haunting spirits.

Characters

Henrietta's Family in 19th Century Bermuda

Henrietta Littenfield – writer of *The Saturday Letters*
Rebecca – Henrietta's mother, married to Walther Littenfield
Mary Sears – Rebecca's mother, an emancipated slave from Barbados
Friedrich Littenfield – Henrietta's paternal grandfather

Henrietta's Family in 19th and 20th Century Gibraltar and Sheerness

Henrietta Silking (née Littenfield)
William Silking – Henrietta's husband
Henry, Frederick (Dick), Ernest and Albert – Henrietta and William's sons
Ada and Eleanor (Ellie) – Henrietta and William's daughters

Henry Silking's Family in 19th and 20th Century London

Henry Silking – William Silking's brother
Charlotte Silking – Henry's wife
Albert – Henry and Charlotte's son
Minnie, Nellie, Violet and Marie – Henry and Charlotte's daughters

Ada Silking's Family in 20th Century Plymouth

Ada Woodford (née Silking)
Albert Woodford – Ada's husband
Cyril – Ada and Albert's son
Edith – Cyril's wife
John – son of Cyril and Edith

Dick Silking's Family in 20th century Portsmouth

Frederick (Dick) Silking
Flo Silking – Dick's wife
Marjorie Dorothea (Thea) – Frederick and Flo's daughter and recipient of Henrietta's letters
Nora – Thea's half-sister

Dear John,

First things first. I introduce myself. I am your great-grandmother. Your grandmother, Ada, is my daughter. As you know, of course, you visit her every Saturday afternoon with your parents. I live in the house just up the hill from hers. Not the one joined on to your grandmother's house, but the next one.

I should say, I did live there. Because, if my plan works out, you will be opening these letters as a young man, aged twenty-one years, and I will no longer be on this earth.

Do you remember seeing a lady at a window waving to you? You were playing ball in the garden, and you weren't sure if you should wave back, but you did grin. Of course you don't remember. For you, it will be sixteen years ago, but for me it is just Saturday last. It makes me sad not to know you. For this reason, I conceive the idea of writing letters. I will write one every Saturday instead of moping and appearing at the window like a mad lady.

You may have a bit of an idea about me, if you cast your mind back. At five years old, you notice things that adults don't expect a child to notice. Ada says you remember the photograph of me that she used to keep on the windowsill. You asked about it when it disappeared. She told you that the glass was broken. Next day, she sat here in my kitchen weeping because she told you a lie. She made up a story when you asked, 'Who is the lady in the picture?' She said it made her feel like Peter denying Jesus when the cock crowed thrice. Denying her own mother. I tell her not to take the Lord's name in vain. It is not her fault. Your grandmother has her reasons.

So, there is a little mystery which I will explain one day. For now, I will begin with the photograph, to put right the lie that your grandmother didn't want to tell.

The photograph was taken on my seventy-fifth birthday and I was pleased with it, just as I was pleased with that whole day. I felt lucky my birthday fell on a Sunday. I've always liked the Lord's Day. First, we went to chapel. Your grandfather, Albert, walked in front with Cyril. Cyril is now your father, of course, but he was only fifteen then. I had your grandmother, Ada, to myself, a rare treat.

Cyril is trying to act grown-up, to match his Sunday suit, but then he forgets, taking uneven steps, now tiny and mincing, now a long stride, then a jump to avoid treading on the lines in the pavement. His father pretends not to notice. I nudge Ada to point it out, but she's in a fluster, adjusting her hat.

The heat is beginning to build, and the chapel has a welcome coolness. Ada eases her little feet out of her shoes and places them on the stone floor. I believe the poor girl's beginning to suffer from the flushes and finding this summer altogether bothersome. She has the tiniest feet, that girl. As if they never grew with the rest of her and have trouble carrying all that tallness.

I sink into the atmosphere of the chapel, the peace and the ritual. I can tell you, it took me a long time to get used to the English way of worship. It felt to me like nothing was happening. But, slowly, I learned to appreciate the effect of the climate on these people. All that greyness takes their energy away. And no wonder. For the greyness penetrates all life. It gets into the food and the clothes and the houses, so no wonder their skin looks grey and their voices grey too. So after a while, I understood that what I took for apathy and deadness was really tiredness. Not just tiredness, but exhaustion, and exhaustion that has got into the blood and been passed down from one generation to the next. I was lucky when I found my husband, William. He didn't have that disease, and I like to think that William and I infused some energy into this tired British stock with our children.

When we get back to the house, I have a mind to ask Albert and Ada to take a photograph to mark the occasion of my birthday. Ada said just as soon as she had the dinner in the oven, and I thought Albert would never emerge from the newspaper. So I sat quietly and upright waiting for them in the living room and taking care not to crumple my skirt. I wanted to look my best, and I was particularly pleased with the stripe in my new blouse. Ada kept carrying on about how I could bear to wear such heavy clothes in the heat, which made me smile.

At last Albert's ready with the camera. The heat is pouring down on me like a hot waterfall and coming up from the ground into my old bones. I'm looking at the plants and thinking if this summer carry on like this, they stand a chance of growing to nearly the same size they would be in Bermuda. I'm thinking I feel warm, truly all-through warm for the first time since I've been in this country, which is well over twenty years. When I came first to Plymouth, I laughed at the little lollipop palm trees they're so proud of here, but on that day of my birthday when I reached seventy-five years, I had the wisdom to feel blessed to have come to the one corner of England warm enough for a palm tree to even think of rattling its leaves.

So that explains the photograph taken in the little garden of the fine house in Garfield Terrace, before your grandparents and I moved up here to these little pebble-dash boxes.

From your affectionate great-grandmother,
Henrietta Silking

I could not of course say to the boy that it is his own mother who is stopping John from seeing me.

Ada comes one day looking as if she wished the earth would swallow her, and she tells me not to visit on Saturdays any more. First, she makes up some nonsense about me finding it difficult to walk down the hill and back – a few yards – even though she considers it fine for me to walk half a mile to chapel the very next morning. At last she spits it out. Her son Cyril's wife says she doesn't want her child to grow up in the shadow of a black great-grandmother. It might become hard for him at school and in making a good career.

As if I go to school with him, nuh! As if I accompany him to his place of employment! I'm ashamed that Cyril didn't stand up for me and the rights of the situation. But I don't want to upset Ada. She dotes on Cyril and on his little son, John, and she doesn't want to risk a rift in the family. I see I have to be the one to suffer the rift.

As to that Edith, who set her cap at my grandson Cyril and stole him away, she has a nerve to lay down the law. Cyril lets her have her way in everything, Ada says. So here am I, on a Saturday afternoon, scratching away with pen and ink instead of sitting with my family, seeing young John and eating a nice piece of cake.

How would it be if we still shared a house, like we used to? Would I be obliged to stay in my bedroom? Albert insisted when we moved out here – into the clean air and the fine view of Mr Brunel's bridge across the River Tamar – that I had a separate house. A separate house, indeed! He said I deserved it after all the years living with them. It was generous of him, I suppose.

I used to feel content in Ada's room amongst all her fine needlepoint – four generations of us sitting in company. Albert has been a good husband to Ada, but an over-strict father. Even now that Cyril's a married man with a son, you can see him shrink in the presence of his own father. I did feel obliged to intervene occasionally. I do like to think that fussy Edith appreciated the few tips on child-rearing I passed on, while little John played with his bricks and charmed us all.

It's ironic. All those years in the wartime when Ada was working as a Voluntary Aid Detachment member (VAD), I was considered fit to meet Cyril from school, baking him cookies and playing him at dominoes. Didn't nobody say I was a bad influence then. We were close-close-close in those days, but now he's grown, he's letting me be cut from his life.

I fold the letter away in a Huntley & Palmers' biscuit tin and stow it at the back of the drawer where I keep my underwear.

Plymouth
Saturday 30th August 1930

Dear John,

Talking about all that heat on that Sunday in Plymouth in my last letter set me thinking about the place I come from. I was born in Bermuda. That's because my mother and my grandmother came there in 1840 to make a new life. They came from Barbados. You have to look on your globe to find Bermuda. That little pink island's so easy to miss in the vast Atlantic Ocean. It's easier to find Barbados, which is a big island in the Caribbean. Go north from Barbados – imagine your finger's a sailing ship taking ten or twelve days to make this voyage with my ancestors on board. How far that is in miles I cannot tell you. Bermuda floats opposite the state of Georgia on the American coast, but a long ways off.

I'll tell the story of my mother and my grandmother another time. For now, I'm remembering the garden on the estate belonging to my grandfather where I often visited. I lived with my parents in the town of Hamilton, and the estate was a few miles away. I'm about five years old, so the year must be 1850…

I screw the top on my pen and stare out of the window. There is the gate of Ada's house. Little John will be there now, being told he must eat a piece of bread and butter before he's allowed a slice of cake. I feel uncomfortable. I'm no longer happy writing my letter to John, and I don't understand why. All I know is, I cannot continue. My plan's not working out.

I go downstairs and set the kettle to boil. There is still warmth in the afternoon sun, and I have positioned my chair in the bay window of the front room so that I catch it at this time of day. As I sip my tea, it comes to me that my discomfort arises from the fact that I'm writing my letters to a small boy or – when he reads them – a young man. At first, that was no problem. But now I'm coming to write about more intimate matters, it begins to trouble me. It does not feel appropriate. How do I know what kind of young man he might turn out to be? He might be like his grandfather, impatient of the concerns of women. I respect Albert, but I have never found him an easy son-in-law.

I would never speak of personal matters to him. It strikes me that one should only write in a letter what one can imagine saying to the face of the recipient. Cheese-on-bread! I'm shocked I have not thought of that before.

So, my plan comes to an end. That makes me sad. I looked forward to writing the Saturday letter almost as much as I used to anticipate the afternoon at Ada's. I put down my cup and saucer and set to straightening the photographs on the side table. All the family are here - my husband and all my children.

Henry, my eldest, is in pride of place in his naval uniform, looking so handsome. Since he died, I do not display his wedding photograph. I no longer need to look upon that woman. My eye falls on the photograph behind Henry - a wedding picture where my granddaughter's a bridesmaid. That Marjorie must be a real beauty. She was only thirteen then, but she'd be quite a young lady by now.

I'm already halfway to the kitchen when I have my idea. I nearly drop my cup and saucer. I will write to Marjorie, nuh! To write to a young woman makes more sense, especially the daughter of my beloved Dick. I like to think I have gathered a little wisdom over the years. Of course. *She's* the person to appreciate that womanly wisdom and use it in her life.

Plymouth
Saturday 6th September 1930

Dear Marjorie Dorothea,

I introduce myself. I'm your grandmother and I'm writing to a little five-year-old girl who came riding in a carriage and captivated me. Your strong character already showed on that occasion. You told me firmly you preferred your name the way I've written it at the top of this letter. Maybe that's now changed. You must let me know. Certainly, you're not a little girl any more. I wonder if you remember that day.

Your father, Dick, was always close to my heart. He was such a dreamer and he took life hard, but eventually he settled and made a good career in the army. A few years back, your mother sent me a photograph of you as bridesmaid at thirteen years old. You look so grown-up and stylish in that picture, it set me to wondering what you plan to do with your life. And so I had the idea to write to you.

It makes me sad that I do not see you. I believe a grandmother has something to say to a granddaughter, some piece of wisdom to pass on, some tip about how to manage in life. Maybe I'm conceited to think that way. But I remember my own grandparents and what a difference they made to me when I was your age.

Portsmouth and Plymouth are too far apart to make visiting easy. Your father has not the habit of writing letters and telling me the family news, but maybe one day I'll sit together with you and your family. Meanwhile, I will write to you about my life, so that you understand where you come from.

It's obvious to me that you will know me better by reading these letters, but I'm not sure why I think it will help me to know you. That's a mystery.

Then I remember: the Lord works in mysterious ways. That gives me courage.

From your affectionate grandmother,
Henrietta Silking

I feel much happier now. I'll take this letter to the post on Monday. During the week, I will look out a copy of that photograph to send to young Marjorie. Next Saturday, I will copy out that story as I wrote it to John, and tell her about her Aunt Ada. I will not, of course, mention the sad situation I find myself in, being excluded from the family visit.

By that time, maybe, I'll have a reply from Marjorie to respond to. That thought gives me a twinge of excitement. Something to look forward to.

Plymouth
Saturday 20th September 1930

Dear Marjorie Dorothea,

I grew up in Bermuda, where I was born. You can find it in your atlas of the world. Get your father to help you. He always loved looking at maps and travelling to far-flung places in his mind.

I lived with my parents in Hamilton, and my father and I often used to visit my maternal grandmother, on the estate belonging to my paternal grandfather, a few miles out of town. This is what I have in mind to write about this week.

I sitting with my grandma in deep shade, under the pepper tree. We shelling peas, a job I both like and not like. I like it for the way my grandma talk as she shuck the peas into the rush basket at our feet, and for the sweet green crunch of the peas. I dislike it for the fat, creamy maggots to be found in some of the pods. She flick them away with her broad thumbnail, but finding one always make me jump and jerk the pod away into the grass, which make Grandma give a deep-throated grunt. She say, 'Hattie, you ain't nuh country child at all!'

One day, I have a question. 'Gran Gran, what does it mean, "mix marriage"?'

She grunt in much the same way and suck her teeth. 'What dey saying to you, pickney, that you come with such a question? Who telling you bout dese tings?'

'The ladies making the sandwiches at the Sunday school tea. They giving me funny looks.'

'Dem two always giving funny looks. Dey so jipsy, always have dey noses in other folk business. Dey can't help giving funny looks, pickney. Dey look so funny.'

I giggle, but Grandma ain't had no smile on her face. 'You ain't answer, Gran Gran. Bout the mix ting.'

'Cheese-on-bread! How do I know what mix dey speak of? Maybe a new recipe and you jus' hear it wrong, nuh.'

Grandma seem cross about the subject of the mix. She muttering on to herself as if I can't hear. 'You ask big questions for a little one. One day when you bigger, you understand dese tings.' Which tell me that the funny looks were indeed meant for me, and that I have more important things than recipes to find out about.

Out loud, Grandma say, 'Give me dat bowl, nuh. You so slow with dem peas. Why don't you run see you granfada? Tell he I send you.'

So I follow the windy path through the thick scent of jasmine to the little house that is my grandfather's workshop and knock. 'Opa? It's me.'

He opens the door and holds up his hand to stop me rushing in. 'Steady! You know the game, little one.'

I should explain that this grandmother and this grandfather are not man and wife. For the grandmother is my mother's mother and the grandfather is my father's father. They just happen to live in the same household on the estate belonging to my grandfather.

Opa have eyes the colour of the blue blue sky. The sun catch on the gold frame of his little round spectacles, just as it catch on the end of his pointy nose, turning it pink. When he's working, he wears a leather apron, worn thin with age, just like him.

Now, he picks a little hand brush off the nail where it hangs by a loop of frayed string and advances on me. I squeak and run behind a bougainvillea bush, but the game is that he catches me and drags me out. I pick up my skirts and pinny and shake them while he flick the brush over my blouse, front, back, sleeves. Next, I cup my hands in the bucket of water beside the door, splashing my face and drying myself with the towel he hold out. Carefully, he cleans the bristles of his brush in the long grass and hangs it back on the hook. The back of the brush is flecked with shiny red patches which show that once it was painted scarlet, and I itch to prise them off with my fingernail. But I wait patiently while he washes his hands and puts back the towel.

At last, he says, 'Gut, gut, good. Not a speck of dust must we have. Come on in. Make the door shut.'

The hut is cool inside its thick stone walls. Light falls from a sloping window in the roof onto a workbench laid out with a regiment of cogs and screws and springs. A dozen timepieces fill a shelf on the end wall. Their precise ticking replaces the lazy garden sounds of bees and leaves.

I sit on my special high stool and set to polishing the watch glasses he gives me. When I've finished, I look on as he squints through his magnifying lens, picking up tiny pieces from the front line of the assembled army and screwing them into place with his miniature tools. He never drops one. This precision matches his clipped speech, with its quirky rhythm, and the vee and zed sounds, which make English sound more interesting.

I have a question that has been buzzing in my head. 'Opa, why does Ma never come with Papa and me to visit with you?'

'What does she tell you for a reason?'

'She say she can only clean the whole house properly when we are out of the way.'

'Then that is why she does not come.'

I make a face and wonder why the grown-ups never answer my questions. They always get vex when I don't answer theirs.

I find so many things to puzzle about. For instance, I know that Opa is my grandfather Littenfield, but why is Mrs Littenfield not my oma? And why do I have to call her Mrs Littenfield, as if she an acquaintance and not family? And why does this not-oma purse up her lips whenever I say, 'Opa'?

Opa straightens up at last and looks at me. 'You are making a miserable face,' he says and takes out his pocket watch. 'It must be time to play the cuckoo clocks. Then must we find your father. Your grandma will have the lunch prepared.'

It's my favourite thing, the playing of Opa's collection of three cuckoo clocks, when I must guess which little bird will fly out first as the hands reach the twelve. I love to see each door flip open amongst its carved leaves. The painted birds dart out so joyfully, flapping wooden wings and opening their beaks to shout their song. But, that day, those cuckoos seem to mock me.

Now I am tired with all that remembering.

From your affectionate grandmother,

Henrietta Littenfield

Today I break my rule and I watch Cyril and his wife and little John arrive at Ada's house, walking up the hill from the bus stop. Cyril's holding John's hand, chatting. John looks up in his father's face, and they both laugh. It does my heart good at the same time as it aches. Edith follows on behind. Who does she think she is, wearing such a frippety hat?

Then it occurs to me that if she would take John by the hand and walk on up to my door to pass the time of day, then I would not be finding fault with her hat.

Plymouth
Saturday 27th September 1930

Dear Marjorie Dorothea,

Many years later – it would have been 1859, when I was fourteen years old – my opa returned to the question I refer to in my last letter. He said I was old enough to talk about grown-up things, but I'd forgotten the question.

'You asked why your mama did not accompany you and your father on these visits. It is because my wife, the second Mrs Littenfield, does not speak to your mama.'

'Why not?'

'She did not approve that my son, your papa, married your mama. She thought he should marry a lady with the same colour skin as himself. None of her business, of course. She is only his stepmother. Mrs Littenfield considers your mama a servant.' He sticks his tongue out and bites in concentration as he positions a tiny spring with the tweezers. 'It is all a load of piffle, of course. Quatsch! Piffle!'

'And for that reason, Gran Gran only sit at lunch with us when Mrs Littenfield's away in the city?'

'Jawohl. That is so. Another load of Quatsch.'

'Because Gran Gran is a servant?'

'Ja, ja, yes, yes.' He sits back and looks at me over the top of his spectacles. 'You have heard of slavery, nicht wahr? They teach you something in school other than the kings and queens of England?'

I nod. Ma and Papa, rather than the teachers, have explained to me about slavery, but I don't want Opa to get diverted onto the topic of the 'piffle of an education system that we have on this island'.

'Your grandma was a slave in Barbados. After emancipation, she came here with your mother, who was then a little girl like you, to make a new life. Bermuda was supposed to be the land of opportunity – which turned out not to be so for those who happened to have black skin.' He shakes his head and gazes out of the window. 'But they were lucky. They had a benefactor, Henrietta Seale, for whom your grandma had worked all her life, up until then. It was Henrietta who taught your mama to read and write. That is why you are named for her.'

'Was she a black lady?'

'No.' He chuckles. 'It was not common for black ladies to own slaves. So, Henrietta gave your grandma money and a letter of introduction to my dear Frieda – that is the first Mrs Littenfield. She and Henrietta Seale had been friends a long time ago and still kept in touch by letter.'

'And that's how Gran Gran come to work for you?'

'Ja. She came as lady's maid to Frieda. She always said it was like home from home, just like the old days. I remember saying to her, "But now you are free, you are not a slave. That is different, nicht wahr?"'

He stares out of the window again.

'You know what she said then, Hattie?' I see his eyes fill with tears. '"Slave or no slave," she said, "it the same, because you treat me like a human being, like your friend. I lucky in Barbados, with Mrs Seale. She treat me well, like you do. Most people not so lucky." Then she said, "Slave, servant, Barbados, Bermuda, the only difference I see that now we free we choose who work us to death." Which, as we know, was the more common experience of her people – fear, pain, early death. You know, little one, I regret that we no longer treat your grandma and your mama like we did then, like we should. My new wife cannot understand it. Shameful, it is.' He banged his fist on the workbench, causing the watch parts to vibrate. 'A load of piffle, that's what it is. And I am a weak old man.'

'But Mrs Littenfield, she allow me to sit at table with you. My skin's not black like Gran Gran's but it's not white.' I hate it that this unpleasant woman carries the same name as me. I was born to it. But she has no right to be spoiling it with her bad attitudes.

'That is because you are my son's daughter. She would not dare cross my son again.'

Opa stands up and waves his hands around his head as if to push the whole conversation away, as if he cannot bear to continue. He goes out the door, scoops up water in his hands from the bucket and empties it over his head. He make a noise like a horse and shake his head and lets the water drip through his hair onto his shirt.

'You have a choice of what you call yourself,' he says, drying his face in the towel. 'Your mother and your grandmother and your maternal grandfather are all Barbadian, which makes you West Indian. Walther, your father, was born of German parents, so you can be European, German. You were born in Bermuda, which means you could call yourself British. You could even be American by geographical location.' He spits out the last option as if it would be unlikely that anyone would want to call themselves American.

'I always think of myself as West Indian,' I say, and then wonder if I've offended him. 'Except when I here. Then I get confuse.'

He laughs. 'Kein Wunder. West Indian is right. That is your root. The mother line is the one that counts.'

Even after all these years, I still miss my opa, my grandfather.

Yours affectionately, your grandmother,
Henrietta Littenfield

I can hardly see to sign my name, and the tears run down my cheeks when I look up. Not just because I miss my opa, although that's certainly true. No. It's because of what happened after I sent Marjorie the photograph. A letter did come, not from Marjorie as I expected but from her mother, Flo, who had opened the letter in error. So she said. She wrote that she would give Marjorie the photograph – I wonder if she has. But she thought it best that I stop writing as Marjorie would find it 'unsettling'. Flo said she didn't want to make it any more difficult for Marge (as she calls her) to find her place in the world. Marge, she said, liked to think she looked the same as other people.

I was so indignant that I tore the letter up. Then I had to piece it together again in order to be sure I read it aright.

'The same as other people.' What nonsense! I stand in front of the photo of Marjorie and laugh out loud. She never will look 'the same as other people'. She is more black and more beautiful. It seems that Flo believes it would make life harder for Marjorie if she knew more about her origins. It makes me wonder what they have told her. It makes me wonder where her father, my son Dick, stands in this affair. Maybe he doesn't even know about my letters. I dare not write to Dick. He might say I was interfering. But I think he would agree with me that knowing where one comes from grows a person roots, makes one strong. If Marjorie's finding life difficult – which Flo implies – then my story, my wisdom, that's just what she needs.

I see no point in carrying on. I spend the days in a gloom and decide I can do nothing. I dare not write to Flo for fear of what I might say. I don't want to upset Dick. They're happy. Flo seemed to me a good wife, a good mother. I did respect her, but now I don't know what to think. It's clear to me that Marjorie will not get the letters I send. So why write them?

But then comes a Saturday of north wind and icy rain, when I find myself sitting at my desk again with pen and ink. It draws me, this writing about the past. I want to do it for myself. The past appears a pleasanter place to spend an afternoon than the present, given the unfortunate attitudes of some members of my family. It's certainly a warmer place. So I continue to write to Marjorie, partly for myself, partly in the hope of one day finding a way to convey the letters to her. Meanwhile, they go in the biscuit tin.

Plymouth
Saturday 8th November 1930

Dear Thea,

I hear this is how you like to be called – your mother wrote to Ada, but said she still calls you Marge. Never mind, mothers are like that. My mother kept on calling me Hattie, long after I left that name behind.

Apparently, you're now working as a milliner and progressing well, although Ada told me you first attended an art college. It interests me because it means you have so much in common with your aunt Ada. She was always very artistic and clever with her fingers. She likes painting and embroidery and making things around the house. Do you remember her bringing you embroidery silks for your ninth birthday?

Ada is also very particular about her hats. Although she does not make them, like you, she likes to trim them up in ingenious ways to suit her taste. So, I think you two have a lot to talk about together. Maybe you could come and stay with Ada in your holiday, and then I, too, would get to see my granddaughter.

Ada says there has been no mention of you having a young man. I think it's good not to be in a hurry to get married. But it puts me in mind of when I met my first young man.

'Last evening, I meet the man I will marry!' That is what I say to my mother on the weekend I meet my William. I know the moment my eyes clap on him. Almost. I know absolutely the moment his eyes clap on mine. I see the same spark dancing that I feel in my eyes, which make my soul fizz.

We meet beside the bandstand at a carol concert in Hamilton, Bermuda in December 1864. We both watching each other and turning away when the other look. I tell myself it the uniform making him look handsome. We young women like to think that gold braid and a red collar with brass buttons don't fool us. But, with him, it different. For all his formal appearance, he look bursting with energy, as if a live human being was hiding inside all that finery.

His eyes appear like amber when the light shine through it. When I find them smiling down at me, I make some foolish remark about being surprised that the army have time to be playing music, when we under threat of war from the Americans in the north. He ain't even laugh. He tek it seriously, like he tek me seriously, seeing past the shy girl and her silly comment.

He explain the importance of music in raising morale, how it vital to celebrate on occasion, and that soldiers cannot be fighting all the time. Finally, he describe the role of the bugler in communicating during battle. Now, you might think I get bored with this account long before he reach the end, but he got a way of explaining things that bring them alive. On that occasion, he give a demonstration of a bugle call which cause the bandmaster to look round in protest, and we move away for fear of diverting the musicians. We talk and talk, and when it get dark, the love light in our eyes show us the way home.

I had a teaching post in Hamilton at that time and used to meet William after work whenever he off-duty.

When I tell Ma I stepping out with a soldier, she wasn't so overjoyed as I. She tell me he will use me and vanish. How can she know when she never set eyes on William? I tell her the army keeping him in Bermuda; he not about to vanish. He's been promoted twice – from gunner to bombardier to corporal and have his sights set on sergeant.

'So you see, he have ambition,' I tell her. 'He know all about the inside workings of a gun and how it can be made more accurate. He set to be a specialist in such things.'

She look at me long and hard. 'Soon, he turning into another kind of spec-i-a-list.' She draw out those syllables with heavy sarcasm. 'Soon, he want to know the inner workings of my daughter. Don't take a six for a nine, Hattie. I don't want you bad behave.'

I protest, but my mother isn't finished with me.

'You always pompasettin' these days. Wearing you good blouse on a weekday.' She shake her head at me. 'You take heed, nuh? You listen to your mother, Hattie. The higher de monkey climb, de more he show he tail. Why you can't go and find a nice teacher in dat school where you work?'

It ain't no use reminding Ma that all the male teachers are ancient, nor do I judge it wise to confess to my excitement that William isn't likely to stay forever in Bermuda. He could be posted anywhere in the wide world. I might go to England. I didn't think I had any further ambition since qualifying as a teacher, but now I have a new one. I want to investigate that wide world for myself.

All I can do is tell Ma that William is a good man. I do not want to grieve her, but the love I feel for him is a powerful thing. I take my dilemma to chapel and introduce William to the good Lord in my prayers and ask Him to straighten the path for us.

Yours affectionately, your grandmother,
Henrietta Silking

As I read through my letter, I notice how easily I fall into the speech patterns of my youth. I hear them in my head, particularly the voices of my mother and grandmother. I could never write down the way they really talked, and if

I could, Thea wouldn't understand. Maybe I should write it all out again in regular English. But it would be a waste, a waste of time and paper.

Dear Thea,

I continue where I left off last week.

In spite of my prayers, the good Lord does not see fit to give William and me a smooth path. He choose instead to teach me a number of lessons which grow me from a child into a woman in a few months.

As I tell you, I meet William in December 1864, and I was walking on air all the way to Christmas. You understand that the winter temperature in Bermuda approximates to summer in this country. So, as we go walking out of town of an evening, we find it pleasant to linger and kiss and do the things that young people do who love each other. At first, I'm careful and decorous and keep myself to myself. But this change as we grow to trust each other more. Your geography will have taught you of the dense vegetation on this island, so you can imagine we experience no difficulty in finding secluded places in amongst the olivewood, snowberry and ferns on the path home.

It turn out my mother was correct in thinking William would want to become expert in the workings of my body. I confess, I find myself equally keen to become familiar with his workings. You are a woman now, Thea, so you understand such things. It feel like a magic time when nothing could go against us, so it ain't occur to me that we doing anything wrong. I still do not regret it.

My mother, however, regret it very much when the truth come out. When I miss my monthly visitation for the second time, I become frantic. My mother cannot not help but be aware, and she guess my trouble. I am weeping and she is ranting, now touching her statue of the black Madonna, now throwing salt over her shoulder. When we both calm down enough to talk some sense, we agree William must be told as soon as possible.

But on the day I set out to do this, William ain't there to meet me at our usual place. He wasn't there the next day nor any day following. He wasn't writing. He wasn't visiting. He wasn't sending me no word. That make me sad enough, but I also had my mother being careful not to say, 'Hattie, my girl, I tell you so.' Instead, the words come popping out from her eyes.

I have to tell Mister Wilber, the headmaster at my school, of my predicament. That kind man say, 'Henrietta, I hoped you would go far within this school, but I cannot keep you on.' I know this. I must leave before my condition show, before gossip start, to avoid the bad example to my pupils.

I know I'm passing a turning point in my life. Before, the path stretched ahead of me, clear-cut, neat and sanded, with grass on either side. That path would lead me to positions of ever greater influence, even perhaps to the head teacher's desk, before which I now stand in a position of no influence whatsoever. As I having these thoughts, Mister Wilber continues to shake my hand, all the while looking upon me as if he watching the final scene of a tragedy by Mister William Shakespeare.

I still din't receive no word from *my* William. He ain't reply to the letter I send, and I have to face the possibility that my mother was right all along. He's a man, a white man, a soldier, and he vanish, just as she predict.

I am haunted by the face of Mister Wilber, looking so disappointed. The path I now stumble upon is far from clear-cut. It's no more than a track in the forest, where I trip over roots and collide with obstacles that loom towards me in the dark.

Just as I think things cannot get worse, the Lord send another trial. He take Grandma Sears from us to live with Him in heaven. I enter the Valley of the Shadow of Death before I even had a chance to escape from the Slough of Despond. My grandma is the one person I could talk to about how I manage the disappearance of William and my swelling belly. Now, I won't have that opportunity.

Unfortunately, as I'm a slender young woman – some are discourteous enough to call me bony – it will soon be possible for people to notice my condition. My friends from chapel shun me, and I stop venturing out, for fear of the malicious looks and verbal insults cast in my direction.

Ma tell me not to fret. 'You wait,' she say. 'When you have a baby for dem no-good friends to coo over, dey soon forget about not speaking to you. Dey just want to rock and pet dat pickney of yours, and each young woman instantly want one of she own, for sure.'

Her words run through my head when I go to bed that night. It occur to me, for the very first time, that when I finish with stumbling along that track through the dark forest, I will have a baby in my arms. A real live human being, dependent upon me. It may seem foolish, but I din't make that connection before, the connection with what going on in my belly.

My opa defended my grandmother more fiercely in death than in her lifetime. He sent Mrs Littenfield to stay with her sister so that my mother and father and I could come and stay in his house, in order to honour Grandma Sears' passing appropriately. Ma, of course, would not let me attend the burial, for fear the baby born with some deformity. Papa laugh at her superstitions, but she pay him no mind.

At that time, I thought I would run out of tears, I weep so much. But at least on the estate, I ain't constantly running to the gate to see whether William in sight, on the path to our house.

Yours affectionately, your grandmother,

Henrietta Silking

I should never have doubted William. We had made a pledge, each to the other. But being surrounded on all sides by doubt, from the parents I'd trusted all my life, it was difficult to be steadfast. William had his faults. No man is perfect. But he was a loyal and thinking man, even if he did love his guns excessively.

Plymouth

Saturday 28th February 1931

Dear Thea,

It is so long since I wrote to you. First came the preparations for Christmas, which Ada and I enjoyed together – shopping, cooking, making presents. As you can imagine, Ada always makes all the decorations for the house and the tree.

We spent a pleasant Christmas Day, attending chapel and cooking a goose. Unfortunately, I then suffered a bout of influenza which kept me abed for several weeks in January. I am only recently restored to my usual strength. I was blessed to receive a fine wool shawl from Ada and Albert, which is keeping me warm as I write.

It's appropriate that I resume my story close to the anniversary of my wedding to the grandfather you never met. He died four years before you were born. If he were still alive, William and I would have been married sixty-six years this month. Instead, he died twenty-two long years ago, leaving me to a lonely old age. But, in 1865, I was a very happy young woman.

So, I get married to my William! We were living in quarters near his barracks in St George's.

It turn out that William had a good reason to stay away all those weeks when I was in such despair. Some soldiers in the barracks fall ill with a fever. In the beginning, he fear it might be the yellow fever, it being only a short time since the fearsome outbreak of last year. He dare not even write a letter for fear it would carry the infection to our house. As soon as it become clear that it was some other disease, William fall ill himself – he laid low with this influenza for some weeks, and then find himself too weak to lift a pen or order his thoughts, let alone travel to see his beloved.

But as soon as he recover, there come a letter that had me dancing round the house and hugging Ma, whether she want it or not. His commanding officer had granted him permission to marry, and William wish this to happen soon, even though he had no inkling of my condition. I tek my turn to say, 'I told you so,' but also without opening my lips. I was concerned about the reception William might receive from my parents. On the heels of the letter come William himself, resolved to meet my parents and ask for my hand. What can they do but ask him in the house? What can they do but like him when he speak so respectfully? And what can they do but love him for making their daughter so

33

happy? All those things applied to Papa. Ma stay quiet with the cooking. She welcome him only with the food she served.

Two days later, she tell me she unhappy that I plan to marry a white man.

'But, Ma! You marry a white man, so why you ain't happy?'

'I say, it's you father dat marry *me*. I wasn't in a place to choose, not like you. So, I wish you could choose a man from hereabouts.'

Then she come to where I was washing dishes, and she took my face in her hands and looked in my eyes. 'William is a good man, nuh?' she say. 'I watch the two of you together. He love you. And I see you love he, too. I just sad he take you away from me.'

Although I contradict her, I know she speak the truth, but I just happy to get the closest thing to a blessing from Ma.

When I next see William, I ask him how he feel about marrying a girl of colour, and indeed what his parents think of it. For I know he wrote to England to tell them of his plan to wed. It turn out that he ain't tell them in so many words. He describe me to them as a "local" girl, but one who was educated and a teacher.

'For that is what is important,' William told me. 'I admit, when I first saw you, I was attracted by your looks. The colour of your skin was so beautiful, I wanted to eat it. But it was what you said that made me want to know you better. We share the same values, your spirit shines through, and, yet, you are also a very practical person. That is why we are marrying.'

It was probably the longest speech I hear William make which did not involve guns, and certainly the greatest compliment he ever give me. I was well satisfied.

The wedding was a small one, but perfect. I notice I had a whole lot more friends after the ceremony than I had before. It seem some girls move their position from shunning me to regarding me with the green eyes of jealousy. I only have eyes for William.

So now I learning the keeping of a house, or at least of one room, which is big enough to be starting off with. And I waiting to find out what's it like to be a mother, while getting to know that baby from the movements he beginning to make.

Yours affectionately, your grandmother,

Henrietta Silking

I set down my pen, remembering the miracle of baby Henry when he finally arrived. I could never decide which was the greater wonder: the pale gold colour of his hair or the silky feel of it.

Papa and Opa were both delighted that he took after their side of the family. I could feel Ma being less delighted, but saying nothing. I could hear her thinking: this just the beginning of a rainbow family which will set tongues wagging wherever Hattie go.

Opa had some years to enjoy little Henry. He'd sit him on his knee in his workshop to watch the cuckoo clocks. But Henry never got to help with the watch glasses, for Opa was taken from us before Henry turned three. The funeral was a tense affair. Clearly, Mrs Littenfield didn't want me there with my blonde child, but she couldn't keep me away.

I never went to the estate again after that. I wonder what happened to the clocks and watches. I expect she set fire to the whole shed.

Dear Thea,

When Henry was five years old, William received a posting to Gibraltar. We sailed on board SS *St Lawrence* in January 1871.

As I leave Bermuda, I see my birthplace as an island for the first time, just as it slides away from me. I've been seeing it all my life, but only from the inside – never from the sea. We leave behind the clatter of the derricks on the coaling wharves, and I take in wooded hills, the grand porticos of Government House, avenues of promenading palm trees, and pale beaches with their neat frill of waves. It all looks so tidy and clean, like a foreign country. I'm light-headed – with astonishment to see it all so beautiful, and with excitement that I'm finally leaving.

There's a tug on my arm, and I smile down at my son. Henry is so fair that folk tend to look from him to me and assume I'm the nursemaid. Back home, I sometimes played a game when I was meeting William in town. If someone gave that look at me and Henry, I would call him pickney and speak to him in the language of my mother and grandmother, all to feed their assumption. Then, when William came, I'd change my tone and greet my husband like a lady, offering him my cheek while I watched those people's reaction.

I stretch my neck and straighten my back, inhaling the tang of tar and seaweed and another sour smell, not yet identified. A flock of cahows are swooping and diving over the bay, starch-white against the sapphire sky, their long tail feathers trailing like they might unravel. I hitch little Henry up onto my hip so that he can grab the rail and get a better view, all the while keeping tight hold of my carpet bag containing all our personal possessions.

This morning, I found my mother's hat tucked into the top of the bag, the soft brown felt she donned for prayers morning and evening. It was always the signal that she was not to be interrupted. The gift of the hat gives me a lot to think about. It tells me how much my mother loves me. It tells me she truly accepts my marriage to a white British soldier, just as she accepted baby Henry with loving arms as soon as she clapped eyes on him. The hat also tells me not to forget my prayers, and that the Lord is always with me. I hear her voice saying it, and I have to put my finger to my eye.

Soon it's time to go below before all the best positions are taken up. William is living and sleeping in the men's quarters, which are better appointed than the areas assigned to women and children. Being a good husband, William has sent a young bombardier, whose name I learn is Jim, to search out a good spot for us, up against a bulkhead so that we have a little more space, and some privacy on one side, at least. Being a sergeant's wife gives me priority, for which I am grateful. The quarters are cramped with little headroom so that even the women have to duck. Jim is bent almost double when he calls me over and helps me spread out our bedding bundle.

Of the sanitary arrangements, the less said, the better. Suffice to say that I quickly discover the source of the sour smell, which becomes a good deal worse than sour as the voyage progresses. The food leaves much to be desired, and the portions meagre. But the galley is well organised with notices about the ration entitlements of men, women and children. We women quickly learn to work the system.

I progress from being wary of the young woman next to me, to nodding, to talking, to friendship. She wants to be friends as soon as she fixes her things in place but, at such close quarters, I'm cautious of being too friendly and then falling out. I always reckon a relationship is like a fire – more reliable if it burns up slowly than if it flares up quickly and dies.

Henry makes it almost impossible not to get friendly. He plays peek-a-boo with her and calls her Auntie Annie. She's married to a corporal, and she's naïve, all the time saying just what enters her head, which makes me laugh. It helps to pass the time.

Soon, the ocean stretches on all sides with no sign of land or other ships. I begin to understand the immensity of the world. The old saying of my mother's, 'the sea ain't got no back door', runs through my head and strikes fear into my heart. It's a relief to see land again, when the coast of England is sighted. In Portsmouth, we have no chance to disembark, and all we see are the docks, which look much the same as the ones in Bermuda. When we leave, I feel like a seasoned traveller and think our voyage will now be over quickly.

I pride myself on how quickly I adapt to the motion of the ship, and find a way of walking that allows me to keep upright on my pins even when the surface beneath my feet takes a dive. But I wake one night and find that nothing is staying upright any more.

The storms come after we've been sailing for two days and we reach the Bay of Biscay. I've been told that the weather's often bad here, but having crossed the Atlantic so easily, I think a bay cannot be worse than an ocean. They should rename it the Bay of Dismay. Gibraltar is in a straight line from Bermuda on the globe, but William told me a whole list of reasons why the ship must sail first to England, and then make us suffer this fearsome Biscay.

The wind gets up in the night, and I think I'm still asleep and having the worst nightmare. I'm not sick but frightened, and obliged to hide my fear for Henry's sake. He is very sick. I brew up bush tea from the herbs Ma gave me for the purpose, and have him drink some. He's soon sleeping most of the time. I did not know it possible for a ship to make such sounds, such crashes and cracks, and still stay in one piece. I expect every moment for the water to come rushing in, and we would be heading for the lifeboats if I were able to stay upright for more than a step.

When the vessel pitches, it's as if she's setting off to the bottom of the ocean – she goes down and down and down before she comes up again. And when she rolls, it seems impossible that she won't turn right over and tip us all out.

Add to that the groans and shrieks of the other passengers and the hollering of the crew, and it's my idea of what hell might be like, except that here is water and stinking slime instead of raging fires. For the slop buckets do not stay upright any more than anything else. I wish we had hammocks like William to lift us clear of the filth. And all the time I'm thinking, 'the sea ain't got no back door'.

I just cram my mother's hat on my head and pray, fit to become a minister.

I give Annie a fright doing that. She looks up and sees the hat and thinks I've turned into a man. It's the one point of humour in those dreadful days, and it kept her laughing until the end of the trip. In between praying, I long for my William and clutch his photograph to my heart. He stands stiff in his uniform and looks embarrassed to be leaning his arm on a fake Grecian pillar in the company of a potted palm. But it shows the clean line of his jaw and long straight nose, and his eyes look at me with something of their clear light.

At last, we sail into calmer waters, and I admire William for his wisdom in choosing to join the army rather than the Royal Navy. As the deck returns to the horizontal, we women start to clean up. I swear I will never set foot on such a vessel again, although it grieves me to rethink the plans to visit my parents, which I made in my ignorance. I had no conception of the distance I would be putting between us. How could I have understood the immensity of all that water and wind and their terrible moods? I can't bear to think of the peaceful life they will be leading at this very moment, doing ordinary things like fetching water and shucking beans.

I hope you enjoy my adventure on the high seas.

Your affectionate grandmother,

Henrietta Silking

All that writing makes me tired and I still shudder at the memory of the storm. I kept to my vow never to embark on another long voyage. It meant that I cut the ties with my homeland, and I never saw my dear parents again.

Plymouth

Saturday 14th March 1931

Dear Thea,

We're still on board that ship, the SS *St Lawrence*.

Jim, the bombardier, skids into our sleeping space, bringing the smell of fresh air in amongst the frowsty bedding. He clicks his heels together, remembering just in time not to salute. 'Ser'nt Silking says to come on deck and see Gibraltar!'

I grab the carpet bag, and we follow Jim who carries the bag up the ladders. Henry wants to try climbing them on his own but his legs are far too short to span each rung. So Jim sets down the bag at the top and reaches down to haul him up as I launch him from below. So we progress up through the decks. I quite expect Henry's arms to be an inch or two longer by the time we reach the top deck.

Jim swings Henry onto his shoulders, and I clutch the bag and try to keep up as he dodges around the sailors running back and forth and the coils of rope everywhere. The noise is overwhelming and I have to concentrate in order not to slip or trip.

When we reach the forward part of the ship, William motions to us from the starboard side. Right up in the prow, the officers' families are gathered. William is evidently the only non-officer who has gained permission for his family to witness the approach to the Rock.

William puts his arm around me. 'The air will do you good, my dear. It stinks of illness down below.'

I am only just in the moment realising the change in the quality of the air. I've become used to the stench in our living quarters where we've been scrabbling about like rabbits in a burrow since the storm. My lungs are expanding in a way they have been unwilling to do for weeks, so it feels as if the air is reaching my fingers and toes.

'I feel better already,' I tell William, and I mean it.

William pulls me in front of him and tells me to lean forward. I look where he is pointing and hold my breath. It is as if a low-burning candle is making a giant shadow of our ship

41

and projecting it onto the wall of the world, so huge is the dark rock that rears up out of the ocean in the dawn light.

'We…are…? We are to…live…on that?' I look up at William, desperate to know that there is some mistake. Surely there is a more hospitable neighbouring island with trees and greenness. But William nods.

I find I'm shaking, and William pulls my shawl higher round my shoulders, mistaking my fear for cold. I am grateful for a squall of wind and rain that causes a flurry of activity on deck. By the time I have William's attention again, everyone's face is wet, whether from rain or tears.

'You see how narrow the straits are here – between Gibraltar and the African coast? It's the gateway to the Mediterranean, and we control it. See the gun emplacements?'

I am not interested in gunnery but, as we draw nearer, signs of habitation appear, buildings clinging to the sheer rock face and clusters of cabins crowding the only flat spaces along the shore. This rock island still looks like a seagoing vessel because the topmost point is smoking like the funnel of a steamship. I am fearing it might erupt at any moment, but William tells me it is only mist. I pray to the Lord that he is correct. High up on the promontory furthest from the mainland of Spain, there is vegetation, but William has been told it is a no-go area where the apes reign supreme. Evidently, these apes who will be our neighbours are accorded the status of citizens. I am curious about this, but William only has eyes for the guns, so I question him about those instead.

It is a behaviour I learned after I gave birth. I had a mind to name the baby after my opa. He was called Friedrich, but I thought to use the English version, Frederick. But then I thought that would be looking to the past. In this new life with my husband, I should be looking to the future in the naming of my firstborn.

So when William came to see me, I said, 'I thought we might call him Henry William.'

When I said that, my William just beamed with pleasure. Henry is William's brother's name. It was like his pride swelled up and split the formality he usually wore like a suit of armour. It was like a lighthouse, this pride, its beam streaming out through the cracks and teaching me a big lesson.

It reminded me of something my grandma Sears said to me when William and I were stepping out and she could see we were serious. 'You soon learn to manage dat man, nuh.'

I asked her why I would want to manage him, and my grandma laughed and laughed till her chair and the whole porch creaked with her shaking. She told me of the saying, '"De hand that rock de cradle rule de world." Dey got that wrong,' she said. 'It's de foot that rock de cradle, while de hand is busy washing clothes and cooking food. But de bit about ruling de world, dat's de truth.'

Now I start to understand how that works, and I see that I am learning to manage my man.

So, take a lesson from an old lady, Thea, for the time when you may take a husband. You must work out the way to manage your man. It is how marriage works.

Your affectionate grandmother,
Henrietta Silking

As I make my way downstairs to put the kettle on, I reflect that to make a marriage work really well, you take it in turns to manage each other. I see that now. I used to think I managed William but, now he's no longer here, I realise how much of the time he was managing me.

Plymouth
Saturday 21st March 1931

Dear Thea,

Happy birthday! You are eighteen today and maybe having a little party and a cake. I hope so. Ada made a pretty card, which we both signed to you earlier in the week. You will receive the card, I'm sure, but not this letter. At least, not yet.

I will resume my story, on dry land, in Gibraltar.

Flat Bastion Road. What a daunting sound that was, when William told me where we had been billeted. He explained the meaning of 'bastion' and talked about gun emplacements until I thought we might be residing underneath one of his precious guns.

Along with other families, we pile our belongings onto the waiting cart. Henry is falling asleep on his little legs by the time we get our allocation. It is dark when we get into this Flat Bastion place, and we have difficulty locating the address. Then we must climb. So many steps. Three flights echo with our footsteps and with the reek of the sanitation on board ship. Have I brought the smell with me in my nose? Or am I doomed to suffer such conditions in the building where I must live? I put it out of my mind along with the scuttle of cockroaches that I hear as we open the door to our tenement.

I cannot begin to say how difficult I found those first weeks in Gibraltar.

The first morning, I wake early, even before little Henry. I creep to the window and my breath is quite taken away. Over to my left, I see mountains looming so close I think I could stretch out my finger and touch them. Yet, from what my William tells me, these mountains are in Africa. Down below, across the rooftops is the harbour, full of ships of all sizes, and on the far side must be Spain. It's strange to be in Europe for the first time and yet to find Africa such a near neighbour.

My fine sense of wonder turns to shock when I discover not only that the water must be hauled in buckets up all the stairs from the street but also that water is rationed. William tells me we are lucky. His rank means we pay good rent for our rooms, which entitles us to more water. I am thinking poor people have as much right to water as we do, but for once I bite back my protest. I am not about to complain about any small advantage we have.

But enough of difficulties. I must try to find some entertainment for you, Thea, and give you a chance to laugh at your grandmother, as many did at the time. I spent much time at the window in those early days, and I see a lady in the tenement building opposite who, every morning, lowers down a basket on a rope. She does this whenever a small boy appears and shouts a word up to her window. Later, he comes again and shouts the same word, so that she lowers the rope, he ties the basket on, and she pulls it up. I wish I had such an arrangement. Day by day, I learn this word: Abuela. I cannot have the arrangement but I think I should like such a fine basket. Next time I am in the market, I go to the stall selling wickerwork and ask the woman there for an 'abuela'. She laughs so much I think she's going to choke. Then she remembers her manners and explains that I have asked for a grandmother. Then I understand that the small boy was calling out 'grandma', not 'basket'. I explain my mistake to the lady on the stall, and she finds me the basket I want. She tells me it is 'una cesta' in Spanish, and we part good friends. So now you have learned some Spanish while you enjoy the joke.

Another thing I learn is to walk right out along the road from Flat Bastion towards Europa Point. That way, I escape from under the heavy cloud, called the levanter, that nearly always sits like smoke on the high rock. It is pleasant to walk amongst wild flowers and breathe again, especially when the breeze blows off the ocean. Another favourite walk is in the Alameda Gardens where there is shade, ponds of golden fish, and elephant trees. Henry likes to sit on the cannons around the statue of the important gentleman whose name I always forget. But there is not often time for such walks as I am fully occupied with shopping, preparing meals and the washing, not to mention cleaning and trying to get on with my neighbours.

One of these, called Mary, lives on the same floor. She's a sweet young thing who sings a lot but has no notion of how to achieve cleanliness. I have to teach her everything, which is worth my while since we are obliged to share the washing and cooking facilities. I cannot believe how Mary sees fit to repay me for this kindness.

One day, I am making a pair of trousers for Henry; he grows so fast. Mary wants to see how I set about this task so that she can do the same for her child. I bought some oranges from the market that morning and set them on the shelf near the window. The two boys are playing with my bag of pegs under the table when a shadow comes. We two look round to see a huge hairy ape swing inside onto my table. He seems to tower to the ceiling, and he looks down, giving us a big stare. Then he takes one orange in his mouth, another in his hand, and swings out and up over the roof and gone. He almost seems to wave us goodbye.

We're both so shocked, we clutch each other, and then we laugh until we have to sit down. But then Mary says, nice as pie, 'One of your relatives dropping by to say hello!' And she's off laughing again – until she sees my face.

Mary has just reminded me of what Mrs Littenfield used to call my beloved grandma Sears. I knew all about Mr Darwin. I'd heard white folks back home who were happy to think that we darkies were descended from apes, while they were busy choosing altogether more dignified ancestors for themselves.

Mary colours up under her peppering of freckles, and now she doesn't know what to do. I solve that problem for her and tell her to leave. I keep my dignity until she's out the door, but then the tears flow – hot angry tears. How dare she? I put Ma's hat on my head, take Henry on my lap and tell him stories about the little boy and his grandmother who lives across the street. Each time she hauls up the basket, Henry has to guess what she finds inside.

I tell my William what Mary said, but he says I have to be patient and it will pass, and that nothing will be gained from him picking a fight with her husband. I know he's right, but I suspect William is more concerned with his reputation and the fact that her husband is twice his size. William doesn't have to endure the children who scratch their armpits and do other monkey antics when I pass. Mary did have the grace to come and apologise, but it must be she who spread the story.

So I accept her apology, but I don't invite her past my door, and I maintain a coolness.

All the time, as I go about my work after that, I am thinking what I can do to rise above such petty thinking and find myself some standing, a place in this strange island society where the military and their families have status but do not properly belong.

Your affectionate grandmother,
Henrietta Silking

By that time, I had fallen into William's way of speaking and used regular English all the time, as I did when I was teaching. But I missed the rhythm and colour of my childhood Bajan. In Gibraltar, I encountered the English language in a number of different hues. William came from the west of England, and his accent was a soft brown. The speech of Mary and the other northerners in the Flat Bastion tenements was incomprehensible to me at first. All I heard was a clash of strident reds and orange. Then there was Scottish, which even William found hard to follow. Here in Plymouth, the speech of local people reminds me of William. The accent is stronger but it has the same soft tone. The Lord has indeed blessed us with a rich and varied language.

Plymouth
Saturday 28th March 1931

Dear Thea,

After those first difficult months, it does not take me long to make my mark in this place. I stop fretting about the ignorant soldiers' wives and turn to the town where I'm always more at home. I find the Wesleyan chapel in Wesley House on Main Street and never look back. I meet a lady who hails from Lancashire, where she was a leading light in the Temperance Movement, persuading men to turn away from the evils of alcohol. This Mrs Preston is busy running what they call The Carpenter's Arms, serving tea and coffee and cakes instead of beer and spirits.

Two things happen which incline me to take a strong interest in this venture. The first is that my William, who rarely drinks more than a small pot of ale, attends a big dinner and falls amongst companions who persuade him to drink a deal of whisky. So much that he ends up in the hospital and fears a black mark on his career record. He is full of shame and remorse, especially when he comes home and hears what I have to say about the matter.

The second thing is not a single incident but a regular state of affairs – the husbands of two families in that Flat Bastion tenement were often coming in the worse for drink, making a commotion in the night and leaving vomit to clear up in the morning. Needless to say, Mary's husband was the worst offender.

My first attempt to help Mrs Preston is to bake a batch of cookies to sell in the lounge. I make the cinnamon cookies taught me by my grandma Sears. All of a sudden, when the spicy smell of those cookies wafts through the tenements, I'm no longer an outcast but the most popular person in the street. The children who mock me come sticking their fingers in the bowl, which Henry is busy scraping out and licking. The mothers are not far behind, sniffing the air as I set the cookies on racks to cool.

'You sure you're happy to eat monkey food?' I say to those children. They shuffle about a bit but take the cookies quick enough when I pass them round. So do the mothers, including Mary, and I'm explaining how to make the dough and we're all the best of friends. I have to bake another batch for Mrs P at Wesley House.

Not long after that, I find Mary in tears in the kitchen, holding a letter she's just received in the mail. I think she has bad news, but eventually I discover she's upset because she fears the worst but cannot discover the nature of it. It seems she never learned her letters.

By now, I'm getting a little more canny than I used to be. I make a bargain with Mary. I tell her if she persuades her husband to come to Wesley House to hear my forthcoming talk with lantern slides about the Temperance Movement, then I will teach her how to read. I tell her William is also going to the talk with a view to taking the Pledge. What can she do but agree? So then I set about convincing William he must come in order to set an example and promote his career.

I work hard on that talk in order to make it both informative and inspiring. My favourite lantern slide involves the concept of the six Ps. It states that the Pledge promotes Prudence, Piety, Patriotism, Perseverance, Prosperity and Progress. All fine goals for any man or woman, don't you think, Thea?

To shorten a long story, where William goes, the other husbands follow, being moved to come forward at the end of the meeting to sign the Pledge, as follows:

'We agree to abstain from all liquors of an intoxicating quality, whether ale, porter, wine or ardent spirits, except as medicines.'

This wins me the respect of even those wives who have not sampled my cookies, and we have more peaceful nights and a cleaner washroom as a result. And now, I like to think I'm quite a leading light at Wesley House, which reminds me of an experience I had in that role.

The story involves a lady of my acquaintance, if "lady" is an appropriate description for such a person. When I look back on the encounter in question, it makes me laugh, but I did not find it funny at the time. It happens not long after we have a new water closet installed at Temperance House. This event causes much celebration amongst us ladies who run the café, and indeed amongst the soldiers' wives who visit there. We all find much to admire in the design of pink roses on the porcelain, the ironwork of the cistern, and the comfort of the polished wooden seat, not to mention the superior hygiene it brings.

So, one day, needing to relieve myself, I find myself approaching the door of this facility when the person in question descends the stairs behind me. She's a new recruit to Mrs Preston's team of helpers, so I turn to converse with her, in the spirit of welcoming her, making her feel at home. She, however, sticks her nose in the air and sweeps past just as I open the door of the water closet. She pushes me aside and, as I start to protest, says, 'I don't care to have your black bottom on that seat before me.'

My breath is quite taken away, and I turn aside into the chapel to sit in silence and calm myself. At first, I burn up all over with the insult. I shake with the shock and shame of it, although when I consider the phrase she uses, I can dismiss her as a vulgar person and not a lady at all. I will call her "Mrs Vulgar". I am also haunted by an unease that has been with me ever since the woman set foot in the café that morning. I now recall she is the wife of William's sergeant major. If I insult her, it will surely have consequences for William. So I do nothing. I hear the flush of the closet. I hear her footsteps ascend the stairs. I emerge from the chapel, and I clean that seat most thoroughly before I sink down upon it.

A week later, I have my revenge without even trying, without being obliged to speak directly to the woman, although speak I did. We hold another Temperance meeting, a small one, attended by wives with their husbands who had been on duty and missed the previous opportunity to sign the Pledge. Mrs Vulgar is there in the audience with Mrs Preston. They have come to serve tea and cakes afterwards. I stand to lead the meeting, outlining the procedure and describing the values of the Movement as before. Out of the corner of my eye, I see Mrs Vulgar becoming most disturbed. She claps a hand over her mouth and, presently, before I am halfway through, she runs from the room as if she might vomit at any moment, slamming the door behind her. I'm pleased to say she never returned to the café, and some months later her husband was posted elsewhere. I never saw her again.

On the subject of Temperance, you may be thankful, Thea, for this activity of mine, because it ensures that all my children grow up in the spirit of Temperance. So you benefit from a family that not only walks in the path of the Lord, but stays free of the evils of alcohol. I commend to you those six Ps that I listed above. They seem to me a good motto for any family.

My life improved further when we moved from the unpleasant tenement in Flat Bastion Road to one of a small group of quarters near the beach. The place is called Rosia, which even sounds more pleasant. What I didn't realise during the voyage across the Atlantic Ocean was that I was expecting again. So now we have a new baby, Frederick, a few weeks old. He just missed being born on All Soul's Day. You notice that my patience has been rewarded, and this child takes his name from my grandfather Friedrich.

Here in Rosia Bay we have more space and our own cooking facilities. There are other children for Henry to play with, and we mothers organise picnics on the beach. Best of all, we are far enough south to be out from under the levanter cloud which used to weigh so heavy on our days in Flat Bastion Road. Sometimes, I feel I have not a care in the world.

Your affectionate grandmother,
Henrietta Silking

I smile at that last line. Little did I know. But as Ma used to say, 'Trouble don't set up like rain.' I could never have predicted what happened next.

Plymouth
Saturday 11th April 1931

Dear Thea,

Last week was Easter, a time of much activity, much sadness and much rejoicing in the services at chapel. So I found myself too tired for the writing of a letter. This week, however, I am ready to resume.

This is the hardest time to write about. Little did I know when I was so happy with our little family in Rosia that things could go so badly wrong. And not just because we moved to live in the domain of the Moorish Castle, back under the levanter cloud. No. Our quarters here are superior because William is progressing well in his career. Maybe that should have given me a clue, because they do say, 'The higher the monkey climb, the more he show he tail.' For the cloud comes from William, not from the weather.

In February of this year, I give birth to our third son. By now I would have welcomed a daughter, but William is happy to have yet another son to swell the ranks of the British Army. Until he meets this new son, that is.

Ernest, for that is what we baptise him, is much darker in his skin tone than Frederick. It is as if we have been working up towards Ernest. First Henry who is very fair; then Frederick who is the colour of honey, a good few shades lighter than me; and now Ernest whose skin tone is more like molasses. When William looks upon him for the first time, his eyes widen and his brow furrows. He turns on me.

'How can this be?' he says. I hear harshness for the first time. 'This cannot be my son.'

That is what he says to me, and I cannot credit the evidence of my ears.

Before I go on, I need to give you a lesson on the subtle and not so subtle grades of skin colour, of which you are probably not aware. Where I come from, if one of your parents is true black and one of them pure white – as it was in my own case – then you are called a mulatto. If a mulatto marries a pure white man – as I did – then our children are called quadroons. If those quadroons go with a white person, their children will be octaroons. It goes on and on, but that is enough.

The thing to note is that, with mulattos and quadroons, the skin tone may favour the colouring of either parent or both in equal measure. God does not keep to one recipe in His use of what some may call the tar brush. For example, I am positioned halfway between my raven-skinned ma and my blonde papa.

Having been to art college, Thea, you will know about primary colours. Imagine God as a painter mixing green on his palette. With this device, we avoid the black and white words that tend to raise the temperature, the heartbeat and the eyebrow. So God has a tube of blue (for me) and a tube of yellow (for William).

For Henry, He takes a big squirt of yellow and no blue at all (even Henry's eyes are hazel like William's). It's as if He's having a joke with us. I hardly thought Henry was my child when I first beheld him, except the pain of birthing him had yet to fade from my body.

For Frederick, He takes the same big splodge of yellow but mixes in a good brushful of blue.

When Ernest comes along, He selects the big squirt from the blue tube and adds a smear of yellow as an afterthought. That's for his hair, which is just as straight as his father's. Except William chooses not to see it.

William, of course, did not grow up with this understanding of how the different types of people mix together. Looked at in that way, how could I blame William for his doubt? But blame him I did. For I felt betrayed. He didn't trust me. He thought I'd gone with some Negro, and if I had not been so sad and angry, I would have laughed to wonder when I had the time or opportunity for such a liaison.

So starts a dark time, as I suckle my child and contemplate the depths and shadows of his skin. Make no mistake, Ernest comes as a shock to me too, having become accustomed to paler babies. He should feel more akin to me than Henry did, but the reaction of my husband and my own surprise somehow slides a layer of separation between me and him. It's as if I stitched an alienating spell into the shawl I'd knitted for him, so we don't reach that together feeling I had with Henry and Frederick. It's always me and him, not us. To overcome it, I try too hard and that makes it worse. So, I end up feeling as guilty as William would like me to feel, but for a different reason.

Looking back on that time, I see the pattern continued into Ernest's childhood – the gap and the guilt and the trying to compensate. It certainly gave me another spell in Mr Bunyan's Slough of Despond. But, by the grace of God, the writing of these letters keeps me from visiting there again now.

Your affectionate grandmother,
Henrietta Silking

Remembering that time, I reflect that life progresses in peaks and troughs. Maybe we appreciate the good times the more for having experienced the bad.

Back then, I became isolated with these thoughts, to the point I feared going a little mad. William spent little time at home, but kept company with his precious guns. He would often refer to his reputation and his career, implying that Ernest and I were a threat to both. I was desolate without my William. He made me feel like a pariah, and I guessed others might share his opinion. I lost all joy in life, spoke to nobody, and wished myself back in Bermuda with my parents or, on bad-bad days, at the bottom of the ocean that separated us, that ocean with no back door.

Dear Thea,

I have a great joy to report. We have a daughter. We call her Ada, and William gives no trouble this time.

You may wonder how this came about. William was distant with me after Ernest was born, but he still claimed his conjugal rights. It is surprising what a man can forget when the urge comes upon him. You may think me indelicate to refer to these things, but if I omit them I deny an important part of marriage. Imagine too that I was not averse to the closeness this brought. It became my way of managing William.

It helps that, for Ada, God reversed the colour-mixing technique He used for Ernest. She is blessed with mostly yellow, but God saw fit to apply the blue to her hair. To this day, she complains that it looks like a piece of knitting.

I rejoice and thank the good Lord for my daughter. I look forward to having an ally in this family of men and boys, in this military society where men have all the outward power. The more I think on that, the more I see how the army relies on the inner power of women, and the wives managing their husbands, to achieve a civilised and sensible society. No wonder they allow the quotas of marriages and provide quarters for the families. The Royal Navy must surely suffer for the lack of such arrangements, with all those men confined together in a ship with no civilising influence.

Your affectionate grandmother,
Henrietta Silking

Ada never did come to terms with her hair. Now it's turning grey, it resembles the wig a judge wears in court.

Sometimes, I imagine she sits in judgment over me. But I tell myself it is only her hair.

Plymouth
Saturday 25th April 1931

Dear Thea,

Three years have passed, and we have another son, Albert. His colouring is much like Frederick's (mostly yellow with some blue), and I make no more visits to the Slough of Despond. We have quarters at the Royal Artillery School, and, as a teacher, I am in my element, doing the job I trained to do in Bermuda. I'll tell you how this came about.

In those bad days, eventually I take my misery to Wesley House. Of course, little Ernest has been baptised and we have been attending chapel regularly. But I have spoken to nobody and have not appeared in the Temperance Café. Mrs Preston welcomes me and tells me how much she has missed me. She suggests I speak to the Reverend privately. This kind gentleman says he has an idea.

He's concerned that most education on the Rock is provided by the Roman Catholic Church. He is therefore keen to support the Protestant teaching of the military school and for the Methodist philosophy and faith to have some representation. He promises to have a word in the right quarter.

I fear William will not approve. But my husband thinks it will give me the chance to redeem my reputation with the authorities. A reputation, I might add, which was never tarnished in the first place. When I am offered a teaching post and accommodation at that school, William is happy to accept. He is by now a master gunner, and he likes the idea of his wife being a teacher, a woman of culture. I will also, of course, be paid, and we now have four children to support.

Now Ada is three years old, I no longer need to manage William. Ada achieves that all by herself and wraps her father round her little finger.

But Ernest turns out bad behave. He is disobedient and goes looking for every mischief in order to jump in it up to the neck. Whenever he finds himself in a situation with a choice between a peaceful and an aggressive action, Ernest always chooses aggression. In contrast to his gentle dreamer of an older brother, he learns early to use his fists. He imagines he must fight for Frederick, even when Frederick has no quarrel with a single soul.

Henry is the clever one. Being thirteen years old, he has graduated to the higher school and excels both in learning and conduct. Frederick is less ambitious, but gains awards for hard work, in contrast to the constant reprimands collected by Ernest.

I am happy to know from Ada that you excelled at school, just like Henry.

Your affectionate grandmother,
Henrietta Silking

I put aside my pen and rub my eyes. It's all so long ago but grieves me still.

I used to dread the times when Frederick gained a commendation and Ernest a detention on the same day, as often happened. For the difference between my boys' intellect and behaviour gave me much food for thought, and still does. It encouraged an idea that I associated with the stories my mother told me of the days of slavery

– that black people were inferior, a convenient belief for the plantation owners who treated their slaves worse than animals. It suggested that being born black meant being born bad. Plenty of white folk, including that Mrs Vulgar and the second Mrs Littenfield, were only too ready to put those two in the same bracket.

I longed for Ernest to win praise, and just as fervently for Frederick to suffer a black mark, in order to dispel the myth.

What disturbs me now, as I fold the letter and put it away, is that so little seems to have changed.

Plymouth
Saturday 2nd May 1931

Dear Thea,

I have a new friend in Gibraltar, an unlikely companion for me, being of the Roman Catholic faith. But, as she says, we all believe in the same God.

It was in 1881 – the July after Albert was born – that I met Consuela. William had gone into Spoleto's for a cigar to celebrate his promotion to warrant officer, a milestone in his career, which had been an important goal for some time. Men have some strange ways of celebrating, but provided he didn't take drink, I did not complain. Evidently, he had quite a conversation with old man Spoleto, who told William that the family had recently taken in a relative and was concerned that she needed befriending. That's what he said. According to William.

I agree to meet the lady in the Alameda Gardens by the statue. I choose that place to avoid a stranger coming to our home. We are living once again in the Moorish Castle. Our quarters are superior, as befits William's rank, but everything we do is subject to scrutiny by our neighbours, which is not to my taste at all. Besides, I like to wheel baby Albert to the gardens in the afternoons, away from the stifling levanter cloud.

On the day in question, young Ernest complains of tummy ache in the morning. Much as I suspect he has an ulterior motive – to avoid some test at school – I give him the benefit of the doubt and keep him home. I wonder if to send word to Consuela cancelling our meeting, but Ernest shows himself hungry and healthy by midday so I resign myself to take him along, hoping he'll not disgrace me by behaving badly. He still enjoys climbing on the cannons, even though he's eight years old, so at least he will be happily occupied.

I wonder how I will know her. I imagine some modest, shy person who is finding it difficult to make friends, and perhaps feeling oppressed by her dependent status in her sister's household. Evidently, she is a widow. So, not knowing how long she has been bereaved, I keep a lookout for someone wearing black or sombre clothing.

Consuela fits none of my expectations. Her arrival leaves me in no doubt about her identity. She announces herself at a hundred paces, advancing in a flurry of scarves and feathers in all the colours of the rainbow. Cheese-on-bread! I hear my mother's voice in my head: 'She come pompasettin'!' But Consuela's greeting is so warm and unaffected that I put all thought of her showing off aside. She embraces me, would pick the sleeping Albert out of his pram if I did not stop her, and pats Ernest on the head, as if he were a favourite nephew. She plays with him around the cannons for a while, giving me time to watch her and size her up. Then she comes and sits beside me.

Consuela knows at least as much about the town and its inhabitants as I do, and certainly does not suffer from any degree of shyness. She tells me of her husband's long illness and of her childhood in Madrid, and presses me to describe my life in Bermuda.

Then she leans in to me and whispers, 'My greatest regret is that my poor husband was unable to give me children. I will love the opportunity to spoil yours.'

She leaves me feeling breathless and doubtful about the fact that we've agreed to meet again the following week.

When William comes home, I challenge him about what old man Spoleto really said, for I cannot see that Consuela has any need of being befriended. I feel indignant that William's put me at risk of making a fool of myself. William just smiles and asks me what I think of her, which I'm still not sure about. I tell him she's very lively and that it's difficult not to like her.

'So she might bring a little colour to your life?' William now inquires, still smiling.

I agree that she certainly would, and become even more indignant that he's teasing me.

'Have you considered that maybe Mr Spoleto was being diplomatic? That this lady might be a little overwhelming to his family? That Mr Spoleto has his son's interests at heart and was looking to find the lady some diversion elsewhere?'

'And have you considered, my husband, that your wife is not so foolish as to fall for all this but can guess quite easily that you told Mr Spoleto that I, Henrietta Silking, was the person in need of a friend?'

'Oh, my dear, you find me out.'

'And does it further occur to you that I might feel patronised and humiliated by such a plan?'

'Did you feel patronised and humiliated by Consuela?'

I have to admit that I did not. William will not see that he's missing the point, but, in truth, I'm touched that he should take such trouble on my behalf when he has so many weighty matters on his mind. For with his promotion, inevitably, come new responsibilities.

So begins my friendship with Consuela, beginnings that she and I laugh over in later years.

It's not surprising to me that I neglect to relate anything about baby Albert, who became known as Bertie, in spite of all my protests. This letter is all about Consuela. Which says everything about their two personalities. Albert came easily into this world; he was an easy infant who cried very little. He continued like this into adulthood. If you put these two into a roomful of people, Consuela would grab the attention of every person there while Bertie would be as if invisible. The only remarkable thing Bertie ever did was to join the Royal Engineers when he left school instead of the Royal Artillery like his brothers. William respected him for this choice – for William's so involved in the fine engineering of those guns that he could call himself as much an engineer as a gunner. But, as Bertie's career progressed, he showed no ambition, which disappointed William.

I think, Thea, that you are not likely to suffer from a lack of ambition. I wish I heard more about what you're currently doing with your life.

Your affectionate grandmother,
Henrietta Silking

Ah, Consuela! I'd love to have her walk in right now. She'd brighten my life and this grey day, that's for sure.

Plymouth
Saturday 6th June 1931

Dear Thea,

Today I move on a year – to little Bertie's first birthday.

By that time, my friend, Consuela, has become a regular visitor to our quarter. The neighbours took quite a fright, I believe, when she first appeared. These wives are mostly from England and have as little to do with the resident Gibraltarians as possible. Maybe it is the English reserve – which appears as arrogance – or maybe they are shy. I think it more likely that they're afraid of the great mix of strange tongues, different races and varied skin colours to be found amongst the townspeople. In the case of Consuela, it is the colour of her clothes that causes the greatest stir.

She is enthusiastic about the little party I organise for Bertie and makes special pastries for the event. Bertie is, of course, too young to understand, but Ernest and Ada expect it and look forward to the cake. Ada gets to blow out the candle. Then I have to light it again for Ernest to do the same, as I prefer this to be a peaceful occasion, unspoilt by him exploding with jealousy.

As I said before, Ernest was combative from his earliest days. He's always getting into scraps to defend his little sister. I try to love his fierceness, his passion for justice, but I find it hard, especially as it strains relations with my neighbours, whose children are often sent flying by that bullet head of his. But on this day, my heart melts. As soon as the candle blowing is over,

Ernest rushes from the room and returns with a package he's wrapped himself and tied with string. He holds it out to Bertie who is sitting on Consuela's lap and gurgles happily in response. Consuela pulls at the string to reveal a miniature trumpet, made of tin and painted with blue and yellow stripes.

'How magnificent! What a pretty thing,' says Consuela. 'You must have saved your pocket money for a long time to buy such a gift.'

Ernest beams and takes the trumpet from her. 'Look, Bertie!' He puts his lips to the mouthpiece and puffs and blows.

It's a totally unsuitable gift for a one-year-old, but I'm touched that Ernest has taken this trouble. In the next half-hour, it becomes clear that he had an ulterior motive. At first, no sound emerges, and I fear that this instrument is a cheap imitation, incapable of being played. Then comes a note. And another. Ernest is so absorbed that he leaves his slice of cake untouched upon his plate, a behaviour I have never observed in him regarding food. At first, I think to insist he finish his tea before demonstrating the trumpet, as good manners dictate, but it is clear that this would be more frustration than he could bear. I'm glad his father is not here to insist and make a scene.

Eventually, Ernest succeeds in making many different notes, and it becomes apparent that he has tunes in his head that he can reproduce on the little tin instrument. It is a wonder to me.

'He has a real talent,' says Consuela, and I have to agree.

In the following weeks, he plays that toy non-stop whenever he's at home and his brothers have not contrived to hide it. To be fair, he always invites little Bertie to listen, and the poor child has no choice.

You may wonder, Thea, why I tell you such a story about an unsuitable gift. Soon you will understand.

In a few weeks, Ernest's birthday comes round. He's nine years old. Consuela becomes very mysterious in the days beforehand, and I guess she's plotting some kind of surprise for Ernest. It turns out that she mentioned his musical efforts to her sister, who disappeared into the attic of their house and came back with a battered leather case containing a full-size trumpet. Consuela then spent days cleaning and polishing it.

'It doesn't look much, and it isn't new, but I thought you might like it,' she says as she hands Ernest the parcel.

He looks a little doubtful about receiving a second-hand gift. Having two older brothers, he has enough of 'second-hand' when it comes to clothing. I hold my breath for fear my son will forget his manners and fail to appear grateful. But all that changes when he opens it. For the first time, my Ernest loses the power of speech. He lifts the shiny brass instrument out of the blue velvet where it lies as if it were a new-laid egg. He puts it to his mouth, and now it's our turn to be speechless. A pure and beautiful sound fills the room. I look from Ernest to Consuela and see we all three have a tear in the eye.

When William comes home, I ask him if he remembers our first meeting at the bandstand. 'You recall how you demonstrated the trumpet call and upset the bandmaster?'

When he nods, I call Ernest in, and he plays his new instrument for his father.

This day is a turning point for Ernest, not only in gaining respect from his father but in his behaviour generally. It seems to me he blows all his frustrations down the pipe of that trumpet and no longer takes them out on the rest of the world.

Meanwhile, William is mightily occupied with preparations for the arrival of a monster gun. He confides in me that this mighty gun is due on the Rock later in the year. It's all supposed to be hush-hush, but he feels obliged to let me know why he will be so busy, arranging its installation. I have not the heart to tell William that I've already got wind that it's called 'the 100-ton gun' from the market people I speak to in Casemates Square.

For the rest of the year, he thinks of nothing else. The responsibility sits heavy on his shoulders, and he works every night on figures and diagrams in his notebook. When the gun arrives at the beginning of December, it turns out to be a great drama to get it ashore. So much so it succeeds in ruining our family Christmas, William is so troubled and taciturn. But he has such attention for detail and cares so much about how things are done that he is to be forgiven for not being capable of chatting lightly about inconsequential things when things weigh heavy on his mind.

Imagine, therefore, his chagrin when he opens the Chronicle and finds the usual lengthy social reports in contrast to a brief mention of his precious gun. He calls me in to witness this scandal.

'Lady Napier's farewell party, Lady Burford Hancock's ball – they get more coverage than a matter of national importance. Listen to this! A gown "trimmed with green beetle wings, and stars of the same worn in the hair, the general effect charming and the toilette universally pronounced quite perfect". What trifling twaddle! And here, less than five lines devoted to the gun. Listen! "The 100-ton gun lately brought out from England on board the government steamer Stanley was yesterday safely transferred from the hold of that vessel to a barge…" For heaven's sake – you know what a problem it was. I told you – the misalignment, the tide, the 100 tons of sand… And that's the sum total of what they have to say.'

If I hear more about the 100 tons of sand, I believe I will go out of my mind.

'Shocking, my dear,' I say. 'You always were of the opinion that the Chronicle is an inferior newspaper. But it's the only one we have.'

As William stages his protest in the living room, Ernest distracts him with questions about the gun. But Ada comes weeping into the kitchen, distraught at the fate of the poor beetles that had been sewn into a lady's gown. She always was soft-hearted.

I notice the Chronicle carries some very full reports, full of technical details, in subsequent days, but William makes no comment.

Your affectionate grandmother,
Henrietta Silking

I count my blessings for having lived a rich life. How different it was then, when I was the centre of the family. Now, that family is scattered and I am on the edge. My children all turned out so differently: Henry, striding ahead, his eye always on some distant goal; Frederick, the quiet one, a good listener attracting loyal friends; Ernest crashing about like a bull at a gate, but always making people laugh; Ada, the artistic one, head down at some craftwork, painting or sewing; and Albert, even at a year old, watching and happy to be included.

While the kettle boils, I rearrange my photographs.

I put the one of myself, taken by Albert on my birthday, in the centre and set my children all around it. A foolish illusion maybe, but it cheers me.

Plymouth
Saturday 11th July 1931

Dear Thea,

You will notice I don't write every Saturday these days. When the weather allows, I enjoy being in the garden. Sometimes, I do a little weeding, or I water the beds if they are dry. Sometimes, I just sit with a cup of tea and listen to the conversation coming from my daughter's garden, two doors away.

The summer in Gibraltar was quite different, becoming very hot and oppressive in July and August. What with the water shortage, the poor sanitation and the overcrowding in the poor parts of the town, it's small wonder that there was always danger of cholera. This is a killer disease, and often threatened from neighbouring Spain in those days. We were fortunate to miss the worst epidemic, which happened some years before we came to the Rock, but we were always in fear of an outbreak in summer.

The year is 1884, and I find myself, once again, in the family way. This was not intended to happen. After all, I will have my fortieth birthday next year. But the stresses on William of installing that great gun were great. When they finally lifted, the relief seemed to go to his head – although it was mostly diverted to another location. Suffice to say, the normal precautions were not taken, with this predictable result. It's the worst time of year to be advanced in pregnancy. I already know that from carrying Ada into September.

Consuela teases me, but I know this is her way of coping with her envy of my condition. I tell her I wish it could be her, not me. But, in truth, I delight in the prospect of another baby. Then, in my eighth month, the worst happens. We hear of cases of cholera confirmed in the town.

We're still living in the domain of the Moorish Castle – which is a ghetto of the healthy. News of civilian deaths reaches the quarters via sentries posted at the town gate. The military keeps itself to itself, a situation which would normally please most Gibraltarians, but which is now viewed with resentment. From the start, soldiers are banned from drinking in the town's public houses or visiting the brothels. As the epidemic takes hold, they are confined to barracks indefinitely.

The only contact with Consuela is by letter. She and her sister venture out as little as possible. She writes: 'The smell on the streets is so vile that we dare not breathe for fear of catching the sickness. My sister says she would rather die than contract such a vulgar disease. She is more afraid of losing her dignity than of dying. The men smoke endless cigars to keep us safe, so we will be kippered instead. We are fortunate to live in a safe part of town. I fear for you having to pass by the patios. Be sure not to linger or breathe deeply in their vicinity. Your time is drawing near, so let us hope the disease abates and allows me to come and assist you.'

I watch the children closely for signs of loose bowels or sickness, and spend a sleepless night when Albert has a tummy ache. I brew bush tea and have him sip it, and the cramps soon subside. But one cannot be too vigilant. We are at least fortunate in the well-run military hospital. It is said that the civilian hospital is in a fearful state.

Passes for essential shopping are granted to us wives on a rota basis. We're only allowed to buy from approved stallholders in the market – those allegedly having no links with the Spanish mainland where the disease is rife. One day, at last, it's my turn to go to market, probably the last chance before my time. I crave green food. The lettuce crop, which I grow every year, is all used up, and the seedlings are wilting and dying for lack of water. We've been pulling them before they are full-grown – limp things with no heart, but luscious to my dry mouth. Fish is banned because several deaths in town followed its consumption, so we're existing on a diet of rice and beans, with occasional treats of ever stringier meat of dubious origin. All the chickens have long vanished into the pot, shared out between the families, so the scant supply of eggs has completely dried up.

Cabbage is on my mind that morning as I heave myself early from my bed to prepare for my expedition. Water must be boiled for the day's consumption. It is an order. Some idea of his commanding officer to prevent the spread of disease.

'Who would know whether we do it or not?' I say.

'I would know,' says William. He's adamant that an order is an order and must be obeyed.

'I'm not in the army. I don't take orders.'

'I am well aware of that, my dear,' says my wise William. 'But where would you be without the army?'

I know full well that, back in Bermuda, I could well be dead of yellow fever. But I have to have the last word. 'And where would you and the army be without me? Without all the wives?'

William just rolls his eyes and laughs. He knows I will boil the water. He knows I'll do much stranger things than that if it might keep the disease from our door.

I find it a joy to be out and about in the town after so many weeks confined. I get to Casemates in good time and move from one pitiful stall to another, without the heart to bargain with the poor creatures who are selling such scanty goods. I fall on a good-sized cabbage seconds before another woman, and we're ready to fight over it before the stallholder intervenes. He's a big man, although his ragged garments are almost falling off him, he is grown so thin. I know him well from buying from him in happier times, and I'm shocked not to recognise him at first. He takes the cabbage and puts it in my bag, sending the other poor woman packing.

Then I set off up the steps to the higher road. Although I have food for six families, it amounts to no more than I used to buy just for ourselves. But my belly has grown so big that walking with my bags causes me great difficulty. The bags feel heavy, I feel heavy, the air feels heavy. The levanter cloud sits overhead and presses down. I'm sweating, and my back begins aching in a way that is horribly familiar. If it's really the beginning of labour, I must get home before anything gets properly started. The steps seem interminable and, just as I reach the top, the pain in my back grips me so that I have to stop and lean on the wall until the spasm passes.

As I gather up the bags again, I hear the approach of a taxi and turn to see if it has room for me. The curtains are tied back, and a gentleman and two ladies are already inside. There is a spare seat so I wave it down. My legs begin to anticipate the joy of having the weight taken off them. The horses begin to slow when the gentleman leans forward and speaks to the cabbie who flicks the reins to urge them on again. I lurch forward in protest, the ladies start back in their seats in alarm, and the cabbie raises his whip. But the taxicab is gone.

I must rest. In order to hide from general view, I slip sideways into an alleyway and lean back against a doorway. My bags fall sideways and spill onto the paving. I don't even care, in that moment, that the hard-won cabbage rolls into the gutter of stinking water that flows past my feet. I cradle the mound of my belly with my hands, feeling it harden with the pain in my back, waiting for it to soften as the contraction fades. I let the weight of my flesh sink, pore by pore, into the ground, allowing the earth to absorb and carry me. I will not think of those animal faces in the taxi. I refuse to feel the tip of the driver's whip on the back of my legs as I turn away. But I cannot stop seeing the hatred in the eyes of the passengers, and I cannot help hearing, over and over in my head, the words of the fine gentleman, 'Keep away, nigger woman!'

The alleyway where I sit leads to one of the notorious patios. Before long, I'm aware of whisperings and snickerings and faces peering round the corner at me. I close my eyes and ignore them. Then there comes the sound of bare feet scampering. I open one eye in time to see a skinny child in rags vanish round the corner. I gather my bags close to me and breathe through another round of pain. It's time to get back to the safety of home. I open both eyes and struggle to my feet. My precious cabbage has gone.

I arrive home in time to deliver my child, another girl, in my own bed. I thank the good Lord that my last child – for surely this will be the last – turns out to be a girl, as well as healthy and perfect. I rejoice in her nature – sunny and contented from the first, but not as passive as Bertie who, even as a three-year-old, allows everyone else to rule his world without protest. She lights up whenever a face appears in her vision, and I see that she will grow into the kind of person who lights up a room when she enters.

I also rejoice in the way William responds to her – as if she casts a spell over him. She's every bit as dark-skinned as Ernest, but this time my husband has no complaint. We name her after William's late mother, whom I never met. Eleanor quickly becomes Ellie. Even I have no objection to this shortening, for Eleanor seems too formal for an infant, especially for my sunshine girl.

But what will the future hold for her, with the threat of cholera all around? William tells me it's under control, that the outbreak was not as widespread as on other occasions, but I don't know whether he says that to calm me or whether it's actually true. Every day I pray to the good Lord not to take any of my children from me.

Those memories are so vivid, I am quite worn out with the writing of them. We must thank the good Lord, Thea, that the causes of cholera are now understood, and we know what to do to avoid it. It turns out that William's CO was right all along.

Your affectionate grandmother,
Henrietta Silking

It's true what I told Thea: that I like to get outside in this summer weather. I have also changed my tactics in regard to my great-grandson John. I have decided to be visible to him. Today, I positioned myself at the front of the house, doing a little weeding as the family walked up the road. I'm sure the boy saw me as I looked over the hedge. I was about to wave, but they were across that road and into Ada's gateway before I could say cheese-on-bread. Sometimes I wonder whether we become invisible in old age?

Plymouth

Saturday 8th August 1931

Dear Thea,

We thanked the good Lord that the cholera outbreak was short-lived. The quarantine was lifted and the threatened closure of the border with Spain did not materialise. We all had a new lease of life.

Now that William has achieved the rank of first-class master gunner, we acquire spacious accommodation in a house in Windmill Hill, away from the levanter cloud. We have a Spanish maid to help with the chores, which is a blessing, once I have taught her my ways. Over and above his rank, William is highly respected for his expertise, and this reflects upon me too. So, I now exceed the status enjoyed by that Mrs Vulgar of years ago, and I like to think I occupy my position with a great deal more dignity and wisdom than she did.

You may wonder what happened to my ambition to see the world. In truth, it's still there, buried under many layers of routine and duty. There is nothing I can do about it. It's not in William's power either – even if he wanted to leave all his precious guns, which he does not. Our lives lie in the control of the military. To console myself, I look upon my family and count the blessings of having six fine children and a loving husband to compensate for travelling the world.

Sometimes Consuela and I take the ferry across the harbour to Algeciras. We feel like children let out of school. We are not prisoners on the Rock, but there is a sense of freedom in visiting the mainland.

'We could board a train and travel to Madrid,' says Consuela. 'We could cross the Pyrenees into France!'

But we settle for shopping in the old town Consuela knows well. She takes me to a tiny shop in a side street crammed with jewel-coloured silks and tempts me to buy. I choose a pearl-grey stripe, but she insists I take a length of crimson chiffon as well.

As we sip coffee in her favourite café, I worry about what William will say to my extravagance.

'He will say his wife looks beautiful,' she tells me, and chatters on about gloves and hats.

I never do wear the crimson silk. It feels altogether too Catholic for me, and I pack it away.

As we carry our purchases back on the ferry, I entertain a fantasy of sailing back across the vast Atlantic to pay my parents a visit. But I never make such a visit, which I regret when I receive news that my mother passed away. She died peacefully in her sleep, just like her mother before her. Papa writes that she had a great deal of pain towards the end, and difficulty in walking, so I think she is glad to be released into the safekeeping of the good Lord.

Frederick enlisted last year. He's stationed here on the Rock, so we see him often. Everyone calls him Dick these days – as his school friends always have. He tells me Frederick is too formal, but I will never get used to it. Henry has been in the army four years, the last two on a posting to Bermuda – a great piece of good fortune as he was able to carry presents to my parents before my dear mother passed on. Meanwhile, Ernest enlisted three years ago as a boy trumpeter. He seemed young at fourteen, but William assures me the discipline is good for him. He, too, is here in Gibraltar, so we see him frequently. The first time I saw my boy marching with the band in the military parade, it brought a tear to my eye.

It is 1890, the year of our silver wedding anniversary. I have in mind to have a grand picnic at Europa Point but, as we were married in February when the weather here is inclement, we decide to wait until September when Henry returns from Bermuda. I will stage an all-in-one celebration – of Henry's return and promotion to sergeant major, our anniversary, and the birthdays of Ada and Frederick (or should I say Dick?).

What a labour it is! Ada, Consuela and I seem to be baking for days. When the day arrives, William sets off on foot with Henry, Dick, Ernest and little Bertie to make camp, leaving the rest of us to follow in the wagonette. William has arranged with the garrison transport officer to have use of this vehicle and driver for the day. Ada, Ellie and I load the picnic and are joined by Consuela who's brought her young niece, Almira, with her. The whole Spoleto family were invited, but Consuela's sister and husband declined due to a prior engagement.

We set off with a rumble of wheels and a jangle of harness, and it feels grand to be seated high above the dust of the road, making a spectacle for our neighbours. I know I look well in my new navy-blue costume and matching hat which dear William insisted I have made for the occasion. Ada is fine in simple muslin. She's embroidered the neckline with pink roses, which match the trim of her bonnet. Consuela is her usual flamboyant self in emerald green, and Ellie looks a picture, but I wonder how long her new pinafore will stay so crisp and white. I tell myself firmly, 'All is vanity.' But I cannot suppress the feeling of pride.

Our feast looks a fine spread when the food is laid out

on white tablecloths. The jellies Ada made are only partially melted, and the cake, magnificently decorated with sugar roses by Consuela, only slightly squashed. During the afternoon, Ada joins her brothers in a game with a shuttlecock, which involves a deal of rushing about, dramatic dives and much laughter. Almira, being much younger and very shy, does not join in and prefers to sit reading in the shade of a tree.

Later, I catch Dick watching her from under his hat. He's leaning against a rock, smoking and unaware of being observed. Then Ada is calling him.

'Dick! Dick! Come and join in. We need a tall person on our side.'

He starts to get up, but not before Henry starts to tease him. 'Don't disturb your brother, Ada. He's busy admiring a certain young lady. I do believe he's smitten.'

Consuela exclaims that Almira is only a child, which causes the poor girl to blush and bury her head in her book. Meanwhile, the game continues.

I don't believe those two exchange a word, but Frederick is withdrawn and moody for days afterwards. Then he gets sent on a maintenance detail to clean the guns in Catalan Bay, and when I next see him, after his return, he's back to his normal self. I think no more of it.

As the day draws to a close and the sun dips towards the ocean, the men start to pack up camp and load the wagonette. With the change in the light, the Rif Mountains seem to float just feet away, as if they're in reach. Strange to think I have lived so long in striking distance of the land of my ancestors and have not visited. William tells me the voyage is not as short as it appears and can be rough, which is enough to put me off.

So Africa remains a mystery to me, beyond what I have learned from the many Moorish people who work here in town.

Your affectionate grandmother,
Henrietta Silking

Today, I saw that Ada was laying tea in the garden. My landing window, which looks across to their lawn, was in need of a clean. So I fetched newspaper and vinegar to give it a shine before I sat down to write. I had a good view, but John was intent on his plate and had his back towards me.

It was not a good idea. It made me feel giddy.

Ada saw me and shook her head fiercely when no one was looking. She will be round here tomorrow telling me not to climb on a chair to clean the window. But it will not be my welfare that concerns her.

Plymouth
Saturday 15th August 1931

Dear Thea,

It is 1894. As the years pass, William begins to think ahead to his retirement, which now looms upon the horizon. We will return to England. "Return" is his word. He forgets I never set foot in the place. But I'm looking forward to seeing a new part of the world, particularly a city like London. William's brother, Henry, has invited us to stay with him until William finds employment and our own accommodation. I already have news from young Henry of this family. Henry took lodging with his uncle while working at the War Office, where he was posted on his return from Bermuda. He describes them as "lively". Unaware of my son's gift for understatement, I look forward to meeting them.

But before we leave, regrettable circumstances unfold, involving your father. In the years since the picnic, he has been back and forth to England on a series of gunnery courses, always returning here.

It all happens on Dick's birthday. It falls on a Saturday, and we arrange to meet him at the ice-cream parlour on Main Street for a celebration. This is more of a treat for Bertie and Ellie, who are excited at the prospect of eating ices. It is a pleasant evening, and many families are parading up and down. As we approach our destination, we encounter the Spoleto family. Old man Spoleto is supported on the arm of his daughter-in-law, Maria. To my surprise, following behind is Dick, with Consuela on one arm and Almira on the other, looking animated and not at all shy.

William greets old man Luigi warmly and takes my arm to present me to Maria Spoleto, a striking and somewhat haughty woman whom I know by sight but have never had occasion to address. He then proceeds to present our children, amid laughter that Dick needs no introduction. William is clearly delighted with the situation.

Amid the cacophony of greetings in both Spanish and English, with occasional exclamations in Italian from old man Luigi, I find myself observing the other conversations being held silently in the gaze of different pairs of eyes. First, I notice the way Dick and Almira look at each other. It reminds me of how William and I were when we first met. She is pretty, a true Spanish señorita with dark curls escaping from her bonnet and an enchanting smile.

William is now inviting the Spoleto family to join us in

ordering ice creams. As I catch the looks exchanged between Dick and Almira, I realise they have planned this all along. Neither Dick nor William, however, notices the other pair of eyes. They are the glinty dark eyes of Maria Spoleto. They looked fiercely upon me when William introduced me, but I took that for the lady's natural manner. She did smile charmingly upon Ada and patronisingly upon Bertie. But when it came to Ellie, who usually melted any heart, Maria positively glared and found reason to turn away and be solicitous of her father-in-law.

Now, as William summons the waiter to secure a table, I watch Maria's eyes sliding from Ellie, to Dick, to Almira. I read her mind as it leaps ahead into a future of wedding photographs and grandchildren: black features amongst those aristocratic Spanish profiles. How she shudders! Faced with the threat of sitting down with us, I watch this lady conceive an urgent need to hurry home with her daughter. Sure enough, she suddenly remembers a previous engagement. She exclaims, 'Oh, the time! What am I thinking of?'

With that, she abandons her poor father-in-law to totter uncertainly on his own. She sweeps forward to take Almira's arm, pulling her sharply from the vicinity of Dick. She fixes him with her steely gaze. 'We are late. Almira is already spoken for, elsewhere.'

She may have been referring to the engagement she's recalled, but the double entendre is clear and, judging from her daughter's dismayed expression, the meaning is not lost on her either. My heart goes out to Dick, left standing in forlorn puzzlement. Ellie drags him to the table, and it's left to the children to rekindle the celebratory mood of our little outing.

I stop writing but don't sign the letter. My heart still breaks to think of the damage done that day. But I can't tell Thea the true course of events. Dick would never forgive me. She would not exist if things had turned out differently for Dick. I stare out of the window. Then I tear the letter across and start again.

I repeat the news of William's retirement and our move to England. Then I reshape the story of Dick and Almira

Plymouth
Saturday 15th August 1931

Dear Thea,

…but before we leave, regrettable circumstances unfold involving your father. In the years since the picnic, he has been back and forth to England on a series of gunnery courses, always returning here.

You will, I am sure, have noticed that your father has a tattoo. In case you wonder, and in case you hear any misleading family myth on the subject, this story explains to you why this 'A' comes to be on his arm.

Henry was correct in his observation at the picnic. Dick did develop feelings for Consuela's niece, Almira. By now she is a young lady, a pretty eighteen-year-old. As their interest in one another grows more serious, it comes to the notice of her parents, who veto the liaison because Dick is not of the Roman Catholic faith. It is no surprise to me. My friendship with Consuela is unusual because of this difference, and, according to Consuela, frowned upon by her sister who has always avoided an encounter with me.

Your father, Dick, being an honourable man, terminated

his relationship with Almira, writing her a long letter explaining his reasons, which Consuela delivered to her. He did not want to cause her pain and unhappiness. Dick himself was broken-hearted. He got himself posted to Sierra Leone, where he contracted the malaria that plagued him for the rest of his life.

Now I see that, without knowing it, he was keeping himself until he would meet your mama and bring you into this world.

I tell you this, Thea, to show your father's strength of character, which you already know. The story also illustrates the difficulties of being a mother and the pitfalls of friendship. There is no substitute for the love of God.

Your affectionate grandmother,
Henrietta Silking

Predictably, Consuela visited me at the earliest opportunity after our encounter with Maria Spoleto.

'Oh, Henrietta! My dear friend, what sadness! ¡Madre mia! I don't believe it.'

But when I asked what we could do for Dick and Almira, she gave a dramatic shrug.

'Maria says that it would be out of the question for Almira to marry a non-Catholic. She has a point. Few people are as liberal in their views as you and I.'

I felt hurt and betrayed. 'You've given up on your niece and her happiness very easily.'

Another shrug. So much for her sadness and her 'Madre mia'.

'Maria is a devout Catholic.'

'That may be true, Consuela,' I said, 'but it's not the only reason. Maria knew Dick was not a Catholic all along,

83

but found it acceptable for him to walk with Almira. It was meeting Ellie that changed her mind, and you know it.'

Consuela paced up and down, fiddling with the front of her dress. She did not contradict me. 'What can I do? She is my sister. Once she makes up her mind, nothing will change it. In any case, I'm dependent upon their goodwill.'

Indignant, I accused her of selfishness. Again, she shrugged and did not contradict me. I told her I would visit her sister, Maria, and demand to know what she found wrong with my son.

Consuela picked up a piece of fabric - needlework that Ada had left on the table. She'd been stitching the beatitudes for cushion covers. '"Blessed are the meek: for they shall inherit the earth,"' Consuela read out. 'So fine, this stitching of Ada's. She's a clever girl. But the earth will certainly never be yours, Henrietta. I admire your spirit. Nevertheless, I would not advise that course of action.'

I was tempted to retaliate about what blessing Consuela might fail to achieve, but could not bring myself to use the Lord's words in this way. Whatever Consuela said, I was not to be deterred from speaking to Maria Spoleto.

'I no longer have to worry about William's career, not now he's retiring. I will stand up for my son, even if you will not. She might be your sister, but how dare she judge—'

She interrupted me. 'Getting on your high horse won't help Dick—'

'What do you mean, "high horse"?'

'Oh, I think you know. As to William's career, do you not think he would have gained a commission if you had not been so prominent?'

I was stung. 'How dare you say such a thing? William did not want a commission. He's never wanted to be an officer. He has only ever wanted to manage guns, not men. He told me so–'

She took hold of my arm. 'Hear me out, Henrietta. I am your friend.'

I was no longer convinced of this and tried to pull away. But Consuela held me close, speaking earnestly. 'You accuse me of being selfish, but haven't you acted out of self-interest – with all your work in the Temperance Movement? Have you once considered that it might have been at William's expense? I have learned something of the army while I have been here, heard whisperings. A wife of colour is one thing, but a wife of colour who insists on being in the limelight, who therefore cannot be ignored, is quite another. Of course these things influence my sister. But she has the good sense not to name them.'

I could not believe what I was hearing from my so-called friend. I told her to leave and not return.

Ada still has that cushion. Whenever I see it, I turn it over. Ada always turns it back with a tutting sound.

Plymouth
Saturday 12th September 1931

Dear Thea,

Today I will write of London. I felt a bubbling excitement to be leaving this Rock that had been our home for over twenty years. But when it came to our departure – November 1894, that was – I was overwhelmed with sadness. The outpourings of regret from many friends (as well as from folk who previously kept their regard for us a secret) fuelled this feeling. I was hurt that Consuela's pride prevented her from coming to say farewell. But, eventually, we boarded the good ship Conqueror and sailed (in calm weather, for which I thanked the good Lord) to Portsmouth. From there, we took the train to London where William's brother, Henry, met us and conveyed us to his house in Camberwell, where I met his wife, his son and four daughters for the first time.

Oh London! Henry told me so much about it, but it is not a place that can be conjured by the imagination. The crowds, the commotion – and the climate! I used to think the humidity in Gibraltar was hard to bear, but this dampness together with the cold does penetrate my very bones. William's, and therefore my, four nieces laugh at me because I can never get warm and am always sending Ellie to fetch me another shawl. It is a truly terrible climate, and only now do I understand how the good Lord has spoilt me all my life. I have had my ration of warm sunshine, and it is now my turn to be swamped forever in fog and rain. It is not just the weather. The thing that struck me most on the journey from the train station was the lack of colour to warm the eye. The pavements are grey, the people grey. Their clothes are sombre, washed out or grimed over. They seem bowed down by the weight of these grey skies.

This household, however, is a remarkable exception. Henry and his wife, Charlotte, give us a warm welcome and make us much at home. They've put a large room at the top of the house at our disposal, with space for William to have a small table as a desk. Ada is put in with Minnie and Nellie. Ellie has a mattress on the floor with Violet and Marie, and little Bertie sleeps on a truckle bed in his big cousin Albert's room. What with two Berties, and an Ellie and a Nellie, we are constantly confused, and the children get some fun out of that. Sometimes, both girls or both boys come when called, sometimes neither.

At first, I welcome the cheerful atmosphere, which contrasts so strongly with the gloom on the streets. The girls seem a delight, and there is never a moment's dullness in this house. They take Ada and Ellie to their hearts, show them round the neighbourhood, and introduce them to their friends. All the time, there is music – with their son, Bertie, practising the fiddle, Nellie and little Marie singing their scales and songs, and Minnie going through her dance routines with Violet on the piano. It's as well Ernest is not here. I doubt a trumpet would harmonise with a violin, let alone the personalities of the players. I'm thankful he's still in Gibraltar. William predicts it is only a matter of time before he is sent to Africa to fight the Boers.

But, after a while, I begin to see through all this laughter and music to the emptiness behind it. What is the purpose? Do these girls ever do anything of a more worthwhile nature?

The shallow words of the songs make me uneasy. I am not one to begrudge anyone their fun, but I begin to wonder whether my sister-in-law is not a little careless of her daughters' morals. When I tactfully inquire, Charlotte tells me they're rehearsing for a pantomime, and I assume this is a chapel event, put on to raise funds for poor children. We did something similar in Gibraltar. I find that reassuring, and I'm happy for Ada and Ellie to assist.

But my head begins to ache with the noise of it all and the commotion on the street outside, with all the carriages and carts and people passing. Gibraltar could also be noisy, but here there is nowhere like the Alameda to go for peace and quiet, and in any case, that would not be pleasant in this fog. William, of course, loves to join in with a song of an evening. Never, I notice, does anyone suggest the singing of a hymn. There is no thought to praise the good Lord for all this good fortune.

Nor is there a thought to thank the Lord for the blessing of food. I see it an achievement on the part of my sister-in-law, Charlotte, to get so many of us all sitting down to a meal together, not least because the lack of chairs mean that the two Berties must fetch stools from other parts of the house. However, I see that as no reason to neglect to say grace. Ada notices my discomfort. She tells me she spoke to her aunt and, the next day, I am invited to say grace. What an exhibition those children make of themselves! The two youngest, Violet and Marie, are audibly sniggering. It causes me to open my eyes, and I see that even Minnie, who is fully eighteen years old, the same age as Ada, has shaking shoulders. What is comical, I ask myself, about thanking the good Lord for giving us food? What shocks me further is that, when we sit down, they receive no reprimand from Charlotte. Maybe it would be different if Henry were present, but his work as a chef means that he is often absent at mealtimes. I see this family need a sterner hand than Charlotte's.

Ada tells me later that my accent is the cause of their mirth. My accent? I who speak a superior English to that which I hear coming from their mouths. William tells me they have an edge of cockney, but it just sounds lazy to me. Evidently, Ada speaks again to her aunt, and they agree that Ada shall say grace in future to spare me this merriment. Spare me, indeed! Charlotte does not think to curb the merriment. I think it is she who spares her children a scolding.

I never thought I would say it but I do so miss the Rock. I miss seeing Dick when he's off-duty. I miss all the chapel folk. Especially the chapel and the Temperance Café. It was my domain.

When William seeks me out in our room that evening, my impatience erupts. 'I don't belong here. I have no purpose unless it is to monitor the morals of this family.'

William has the nerve to laugh and takes care to remind me that it is not my place to do so. 'I don't think that would go down too well.'

He tries to embrace me but the smell of porter is on his breath.

'You are no better,' I say. 'Some example to our children!'

'I take one small pot of ale with my brother, and that is a sin?'

I push him away. 'I thought to have your support, at least. But I see I am quite alone.'

William leaves the room, and I weep as I listen to his steps on the stairs. Who is this man who is a stranger to me?

You see, Thea, marriage is all about weathering the bad times and remembering the good.

Your affectionate grandmother,
Henrietta Silking

I'm in turmoil when I put down my pen. It was a turbulent time for me. I missed Gibraltar more than I could say. It was more than missing those people. It was as if the very rock, the earth of the place, pulled me back. I felt it as I left that

89

day and looked back – and up and up at that sheer face of rock. So often I'd found it oppressive, as if it were bearing down on me. But, on that day, I felt it had protected me. The tears came to my eyes and I had to look out to sea to compose myself. I would not say such foolish things to anyone. It is the good Lord, of course, and not a piece of limestone that protects me.

I hoped to be going to lodge briefly with sympathetic family, and so it seemed at first. But soon I was more at sea than on the ocean passage to England. I'd lost my way. It put me in mind of when I arrived in Gibraltar, in Flat Bastion Road. But then I was a young woman, full of energy and hope. In London, I felt my age and more. I did pray, but no answers came.

Now I am even older, in a similar position, and ashamed that my faith is not strong enough to give me hope.

Plymouth
Saturday 3rd October 1931

Dear Thea,

Following on from the unease I felt in this household of our kind relatives, I took comfort from the fact that at least this family went regularly to chapel. If you can call it regular, when one or two of the girls often do not attend because they are required to rehearse.

On one such occasion, I expressed surprise to Charlotte that rehearsals should be organised on the Lord's Day, let alone at times that clashed with attendance at chapel. She replied that this was not surprising since there was no connection between the pantomime and chapel. She seemed a little guarded in her answer, which convinced me there was more to this story. I resolved to pursue it when I had the opportunity.

So, next afternoon, when Charlotte and I are sitting with our mending beside the range, I broach the subject.

'Your girls seem to work so hard at their frivolity, I wonder—'

I get no further. Charlotte drops the sock she is darning, with no thought to where the needle might fall, and stares at me. Indignant, she says, 'Frivolity? That is their living you are speaking of. They work very hard, my girls.'

'Their living?'

'Why, yes. They earn good money for their talents, and they work at being the best in their field.'

'They are paid to dance and sing?'

'What do you imagine? That a London theatre can obtain their services for nothing? That they walk on stage for fun?'

I take a deep breath to conceal my shock. 'I was under a misapprehension,' I say. 'I was imagining they work for charity.'

'That would not put bread on the table. That would not allow me to reduce my work of tie-making and save my poor eyes from ruination. Minnie and Nellie are professionals, Henrietta. How else do you think they came to go to New York last year? Indispensable to the success of the show, they were.'

'New York? I had no idea…' I am lost for words and we sew in silence until I find an excuse to repair to our room.

William, of course, knows all about the trip to New York, but has not seen fit to tell me. He claims it slipped his mind. He tells me that the girls are involved not just with pantomime but with music hall performance in general. That makes me shudder, for I have heard about the iniquities involved in such a life. But William sees nothing wrong in that. He sees nothing wrong with missing chapel 'occasionally'. Just as he sees nothing wrong with taking 'a glass of porter' alongside playing a game of billiards with his brother.

After one such evening when the two of them come home, William announces, 'Henrietta is cross. Once again, I've broken the Pledge. But I'm unrepentant!'

I feel betrayed. He has often broken it and I have always forgiven him. Now, he starts dancing Charlotte round the kitchen table. Henry bows low and asks me to do him a similar honour. They are both mocking me.

I'm about to decline when William says, 'For once, my dear, show Henry and Charlotte that you are happy to be here.'

What can I do then but accept? I find myself quite out of breath, but it does lighten the mood.

It strikes me that we have lived a very sheltered life, surrounded by the military, in Gibraltar. I don't like the feeling that everything is now spinning out of control. The William I've been married to for close on thirty years has vanished since he came to England and kept company with his brother. He's a different person without the context of the army. It's as if we never knew each other.

Next day, Charlotte says, 'So you were involved with the Temperance Movement in Gibraltar?'

I nod, wary of what is to come.

'Henry tells me William is proud of what you achieved.'

I'm relieved, and we discuss the evils of drink, mostly suffered by women and children.

Then Charlotte says, 'But there is no harm in moderation. Over-indulgence is ugly. But so is excessive self-denial, wouldn't you agree? There's nothing temperate about being obsessed with abstinence and giving up on pleasure. We tend to muddle along in the middle. That is what I call temperance.'

'I certainly am no killjoy.'

She ignores me. 'After all, we're in the business of pleasure. Which reminds me, I want to reassure you, Henrietta, that I take the girls' reputation very seriously. Everything at the theatre is conducted in the best possible taste, with the greatest decorum, and they are chaperoned at all times.'

'But in New York? How could you be sure?'

'There is a woman whose job it is to take charge of the girls, to supervise them at all times, to find suitable lodging, to escort them. Really, Henrietta, do you imagine I sent them off to America with no safeguards?' She gives me no time to reply. 'And before you give me Matthew 6:24, "Ye cannot serve God and mammon"...'

As if I would!

'...let me give you Matthew 25, the parable of the talents.' She laughs, as if trying to make this into a joke. 'You see, I can trade scriptures with you. Had it all my childhood. You can have too much of a good thing.'

I don't agree, but by now she is quite pink. I fear I've implied too much criticism of her as a mother and seek to make amends. 'Forgive me, Charlotte. I am sure you know what you are doing. It is all a strange new world to me.'

Which is the truth.

A coolness develops between myself and Charlotte after that. As if to counteract it, Ada spends a lot of time with her aunt learning how to make the ties that Charlotte sews for a store in Knightsbridge. At the same time, Ellie asks Marie to teach her some dance routines, and cousin Bertie starts to teach young Bertie to play his fiddle, which is not pleasing to the ear. I feel isolated and take refuge in my Bible.

In our room, I weep with frustration, I feel so alone.

William talks gently to me. 'My dear, might you not try to join in a little? Might you take a turn playing the piano for little Marie when Violet is tired of it? Would that be so very difficult?'

I shake my head. 'How can I encourage it? All the singing and dancing. Those girls always pompasettin'—'

'No, my dear. Not pompasetting, not showing off. But rehearsing. Now—'

'And on the stage? Flaunting themselves?'

'Not flaunting, but performing. Performing in a professional manner. Now, as I was saying, could you not take an interest?'

I tell him I will try.

'And, my dear, I know it is of solace to you, but I suggest you leave the Bible here in our room. It tends to create a bad atmosphere when you sit reading and murmuring texts aloud.'

I tell him I'm no mad old woman, muttering aloud to herself. Even if I did let slip the odd word, I fail to understand how the word of the good Lord can make a bad atmosphere.

'It is just that it can be taken as criticism, reproach. I would prefer to show appreciation of the kindness my brother and his family have shown us.'

'I am not an ungrateful woman, but I am weary of all the ungodly activities in this household. I just wish we could find our own place.'

'Come January, Henry will set about helping me with that. As he said, there is only seasonal work available now. The time is not right.'

I take William's advice. I help Charlotte with the making of pies and puddings for Christmas, and eventually I notice a thawing of her manner. She is a good-hearted woman, for all her shortcomings. I come to enjoy the cooking, and I'm further uplifted by the news that both Henry and Ernest have Christmas leave and will spend the day with us.

The growing warmth between Ada and Charlotte still concerns me, as well as the amount of time Ada spends gossiping with Minnie or playing duets with Violet. On the one hand, I'm happy for her; on the other, I fear the long-term influence of their values. It is impossible to interfere between the girls, but I find a way to have Ada at my side. I set her to writing out her favourite beatitudes and decorating them prettily. We will stick them into the Christmas cards we plan to send. She takes great care, adorning them with her signature scrolls and leaves that her cousins admire so much.

Christmas brings its own challenges. Drink is brought into the house. Evidently, it is the custom to partake on this day, the occasion of the Lord's birthday, when it feels to me even less appropriate than at any other time. I decline, of course. Charlotte quickly becomes quite red in the face, and not just from the heat of the range. I know the new William will join his brother in a jug of porter, but I'm not prepared for how much he drinks, and not just ale but brandy too. Again, I feel betrayed. William, as the older brother, should be setting an example, but instead he is showing off. And what of the example Charlotte should be setting to her girls?

Ada is offered a glass. I'm grateful when she refuses and comes to sit by me.

*

As promised, in the new year, Henry puts himself out to give William introductions to a number of his business acquaintances, so we hope it will not be long before he finds a position. I impress upon him the need to get out of London. He is abrupt with me. 'Beggars can't be choosers' is all he says.

Meanwhile, young Bertie has enlisted with the Royal Engineers. The passivity of his childhood has turned into a quiet determination and, while I will miss his presence, I am proud that he is making a career for himself.

The final humiliation comes when William finds a job. Of all things, he takes a position as a brewer's agent in a place called Sheerness. He secures it through a gentleman who comes regularly to the hotel where Henry works. Has he done this to spite me? Or to prove to his brother that he is in control and not me?

William sighs impatiently. 'It's well paid. It comes with a house. It's well away from my generous relations. What more do you want?' He gives me a fierce stare. 'You should be counting your blessings.' With that, he leaves the room.

Certainly, one blessing is the prospect of moving out of Henry's household and settling in our own home. Little did I know what lay in store.

I write of all this, Thea, to show you how vigilant one must be. Years later, we heard that Violet continued to perform and, indeed, married an actor. Her children must by now be of your age or close. I lost touch with that branch of the family after William died, you understand. But suffice it to say, if it should ever arise, I would advise you against consorting with those particular cousins.

Your affectionate grandmother,
Henrietta Silking

How I missed Consuela at that time. I was so alone and had no friend to confide in. I even wrote a letter to her, but tore it up. My pride would not allow me to post it, so bitter was our last encounter. I regret that now – both my arrogance and the loss of a valued friend. But at the time, I was hurt by the alacrity with which Consuela turned against me and closed ranks with her family. I did visit Maria Spoleto. I was not on any 'high horse', but nevertheless, suffice it to say, it was not a satisfactory interview.

Plymouth
Saturday 17th October 1931

Dear Thea,

This week, Thea, you will find us – Ada, Ellie and me – on our way to a new life in Sheerness.

The train clatters on through a wasteland, the smoke swirling past the window barely visible against frosted marshland and fields rigid with frozen water. Even the grass beside the track is spiked with ice.

So this is England's green and pleasant land, I think, wondering where I heard that phrase and who was bent on deceiving me. I use my handkerchief to clean the window. It comes away black with grime, but clearing the glass makes no difference anyway. The mist inside the carriage is negligible compared with the fog outside. Occasionally, a fencepost looms and recedes or the cloud lifts enough to reveal scrubby vegetation white as sugar.

But mostly my gaze wanders untethered in that desert beyond the window – there are no reference points – until my eyes seem to play tricks on me. A cloud makes a beckoning finger, and a series of black posts, stark against the white-out, are skeletons, a procession of spirit ancestors in the underworld, the fearsome duppies of my childhood.

Before I can rebuke myself for such superstitious fancies, or fasten on a line of scripture for comfort, a saying of my grandfather's drops into my consciousness: 'Underneath the skin, black people, white people, we all have red blood and white bones. Good people, bad people, happy people, sad people, people who judge, people who get judged – all simply human beings.'

Why is Opa coming back to haunt me at this time? The picture of his workshop with its neatly regimented watch parts and ticking clocks floats beyond the window in place of the bleak landscape. So long ago. So far away. I was another person then. I am not the person that child expected to grow into.

The train jolts suddenly, and I'm distracted as Ada startles awake. When I glance back outside, the vision has gone. I am surprised it hasn't melted a workshop-shaped glow into the marshland. There is a shift in the train's clackety-clack rhythm and it wheezes and shudders to a stop. Surely, this isn't it. I peer into the dense greyness but can see nothing, certainly no sign of a town. I try to stay composed, adjusting my hat. Just in case. A lady must always be prepared.

Ada is sleeping again, in a perfectly upright position with Ellie sprawled across her lap. My, oh my, what that child gets away with. At least it is peaceful without Ellie's constant chatter. I set to wondering about the house that William has waiting for us. How will I dry clothes in this dank and dripping place? For once, I am grateful to Charlotte and her maid for the lessons they taught me about keeping house in England where the sun is not to be relied upon.

Before I left Camberwell, I placed a text on the pillow of each member of the family. It didn't take me long once they were all assembled in the hall to bid us farewell. The texts were left over from those Ada fashioned to enclose with our Christmas cards. The younger cousins will laugh and admire Ada's scrollwork. Charlotte will sniff, and Henry will shrug. Minnie will be disappointed in her pious cousin, and may not keep her promise to write every day. Ada will keep writing for a while and then conclude that Minnie is too busy or has forgotten her. She will give up the plan to 'visit often'. You, Thea, may think I am unkind to interfere in a friendship in this way, but when you become a mother, you will understand how protecting your child must come first.

A flicker of shadow makes me glance back at the window. A shaft of sun has broken through the fog and falls across three skeletal trees branching like coral in moonlight.

'What are you smiling at, Mama?' Ada has woken and is pressing her face to the window to see further down the track.

I gesture towards the sentinel trees. 'Hope springs eternal. They stand there like guardian angels.'

'Hoar frost,' says Ada, stroking Ellie's hair and tickling her to wake her up. 'In Camberwell, the fog was just dirty. This is beautiful.'

'Providing you're sitting in a warm railway carriage. Even if it is filthy.' I hold out my blackened handkerchief, and Ada makes a face and moves her arm away from the window frame.

'Where are we?' Ellie stretches and rubs her eyes.

'Come here, child, and let me smooth your skirt.' I shake out the crumpled folds of her dress and iron the creases with the flats of my hands. 'Now, sit up and see where we're going to be living.'

Ellie bounces onto the seat and leans over Ada to look out. 'But it's still the white dark.'

The fog has closed in again and the trees have vanished.

'Your angels have flown away,' says Ada.

'What angels?'

'Mama said the trees looked like angels.'

Ellie peers into the mist. 'There aren't any trees.'

'They're hiding in the fog.'

'Maybe they've flown away to heaven. Maybe heaven is like this, everything made of clouds.' Ellie giggles. 'Maybe we are in heaven really.'

Ada smiles over Ellie's head, but I say nothing. I have higher hopes of heaven than an English fog, and fear that this climate is to be a severe test of my faith. The more I see of this grey country and the more its dankness penetrates my bones, the more I feel a fleeting attraction to the warmth of hellfire. Such is temptation. May I be forgiven for having such a thought, even for a moment. Pilgrims in a barren land, that's what we are.

Aloud, I say, 'We don't yet deserve to find us in heaven. The good Lord is sending us to Sheerness. No doubt, he has something to teach us here.'

It turned out that Sheerness had a great deal to teach us.

Your affectionate grandmother,

Henrietta Silking

Sometimes I wonder why I am engaged in this writing of letters. One memory ripples into another in unpredictable ways. The ripples make waves and stir up a whirlpool. That, in its turn, churns up all manner of manifestations on the seabed of the past that would be better left buried. It all moves beyond my control and disturbs me in ways that are not alleviated by a cup of tea. It is fortunate that I have chapel to look forward to tomorrow morning.

Plymouth
Saturday 24th October 1931

Dear Thea,

My first disappointment in Sheerness concerned our home – which was situated next door to a public house. My William had not thought to inform me of this. Which is to say, he had no doubt thought of it and deemed it wiser to keep quiet. I did not take long to put him right on that matter. It is a weakness common in a husband to imagine his wife will not notice a thing, simply because he wishes her not to. Of course, William was at pains to point out that both the house and the tavern belonged to the brewery. He reminded me at length of the fact that he was employed by the said brewery and that this explained why the yard at the back, instead of being laid to grass and beds for growing vegetables, was given over to the storage of kegs and crates containing ale. William told me this was a condition of our tenancy, not for discussion. However, William soon understood that this was a matter for a good deal of discussion.

As you go through life, Thea, you will learn to make choices about which situations to simply ignore, which are suitable for compromise, and which require you to take a stand.

The house itself is adequate. It is dry and light and allows for Ada and Ellie to have a bedroom each, with a tiny attic for when the boys come home on leave. William has done well in getting a girl to thoroughly clean it. I spend the first week unpacking our boxes, rearranging the furniture, and listing what we need to make the place into a comfortable home. I am happy for Ada and Ellie to explore the neighbourhood, leaving me free to set things up without interference.

I write a formal note to my sister-in-law, thanking her for taking us in for such an extended period, and receive a reply within a day. She asks me to thank Ada for the 'charming messages left behind for each of us'. I can almost hear the sniff coming off the notepaper. She goes on to congratulate me on this 'wise and charming daughter'. She encloses a note from Violet addressed to Ada. To my surprise, Violet writes that she and her sisters were enchanted with the special sayings Ada left behind and that 'the Bible seems more interesting when you speak about it than when the Minister preaches'. I am, of course, pleased at the Bible gaining favour, in spite of Violet's irreverence for the Minister. But it is not the result I intended. Violet finishes: 'I miss you, we had such fun.' This contrasts with Charlotte who adds a text after her signature: Matthew 7:1. She doesn't have to add, 'Judge not, that ye be not judged.' I feel judged indeed.

Next day, I am out shopping when the afternoon post comes. On my return, Ada is full of letters she has received from Minnie and Nellie.

'They write that I gave them all a text before we left – the ones with the scrollwork I made at Christmas. It was neither Ellie nor I, so it must have been you, Mama. When did you do it? I did not notice.'

'I thought it would be a suitable parting gift. And I knew you would be too modest to do it yourself.'

'That was very kind, to be sure,' says Ada, but she has

such an edge on her voice that I look at her sharply. I am not used to such a tone. In Gibraltar, Ada was always so biddable, a home-loving creature who never pushed herself forward. It confirms my instinct to put a distance between her and her cousins. So I tell her firmly that it would be unwise to enter into a correspondence with Minnie.

To my surprise, she laughs. 'Why would you say that, Mama?'

'You know quite well what I think of those girls and the way they are allowed to carry on. As I've said before, "The higher the monkey climb, the more he show he tail."'

'Oh, Mama! That old saying. This isn't about showing off. It's what Minnie and Nellie do for a living.'

'And what sort of a living is that? Pompasettin' is what it is. Making an exhibition of themselves! Not something I'd want to see my daughter doing.'

'Well, the way I see it, Mama, they use their talents, their singing and dancing, to make people happy. People who are worn out with hard work forget their worries for an hour or two, and see some colour in their life, enjoy it, join in, sing and clap and laugh.'

'You seem to know a great deal about it for one who has never attended such a performance.'

'We talked a lot about it. Our cousins are not as unthinking as you believe, Mama. Anyway, I didn't know you had attended a show yourself.'

'Don't be cheeky. As you know, I would never set foot in such a place. And don't you be telling me my opinion of our relations. But I read the newspapers. I'll have you know, Ada, those theatres are frequented by men of no morals, stage door Johnnies, they're called. They prey on the girls, bribe them with jewels, take advantage of them. But if the girl falls pregnant, they vanish, abandon them to the workhouse. Poor, foolish girls.'

'But Minnie and Violet—'

'Of course, not them. But, I'm saying, it is not a wholesome environment. As to folk losing their cares, they would be better attending chapel and laying their problems before the good Lord.'

'Of course, Mama. But do you know? When we came to Camberwell from Gibraltar, I felt like – how can I describe it – like a horse kept in a stable all winter that is let out into a green meadow where it can gallop and gallop. You know, all those fields of wild flowers, like we saw on the railway posters.'

I'm so surprised that I say nothing.

'We were so cooped up all those years on the Rock. You do understand, Mama?'

I think I understand only too well. 'Enough, child,' I say. 'Now, remember what I said about keeping in touch with that Minnie.'

Ada readily agrees, so I think maybe she is a little chastened. But then she says, 'Minnie tells me that Violet sent me a note, enclosed in her mama's letter to you. I didn't know you had a letter from Aunt Charlotte.'

'You do not know everything,' I reply, hearing once again an edge of impertinence in her voice. I choose not to read out Charlotte's letter for fear my daughter adds the sin of pride to that of impudence. I am, however, obliged to give her Violet's note which, of course, I always intended to do. Ada immediately sets about replying to it.

I am churned up – by Ada's manner, by Charlotte's letter. I must get out of the house. I dress for the inclement weather, pulling on my mother's old hat that I used to wear for gardening in Gibraltar. I take my shawl over my head to keep the hat on and tie it firmly round my shoulders. It is well I take such precautions. As I step out of the shelter of the buildings onto the shore road, I'm knocked sideways by the force of the wind and struggle to hold my balance. No one else has ventured abroad. I am alone.

I set off into the gale, watching the white crests of waves in the estuary, which looks like the open sea. Strange to think that this cold mass of water joins with the English Channel and then with the Atlantic Ocean, stretching all the way to Bermuda. I think of my warm native island, but my imagination refuses to conjure any heat. The gale flays the skin from my face and the waves roll in as if they would keep on coming and break right over me.

I'm a tiny speck in the vastness, battling through the elements. So far in time and space from me and William courting in Bermuda. Love amongst the snowberries. Full of hope and certainty. Now, I am stripped of any wisdom, of any hope for the future. This wasteland has frozen the warmth between William and me. I see the sad face of Mister Wilber, my head teacher in Bermuda. I chose William over my teaching career, and now there is nothing. Wisdom, William, all washed away. God is telling me how insignificant I am.

Then comes the rain. My face becomes a pincushion for a barrage of icy needles. The screaming gulls seem to sound a warning. It is time to turn for home, to my children. That is where I have significance. That is where I am needed.

Ada and Ellie have brought news that there is a thriving Wesleyan community in Sheerness, and I look forward to us all attending chapel on Sunday. It will be a good way to begin our return to a normal family life.

Your affectionate grandmother,
Henrietta Silking

I have not told Thea exactly what happened on my walk. I did not turn voluntarily for home. No. The gulls I thought I was hearing turned out to be William, yelling into the gale. He took my arm and turned me round. We seemed to fly home with the storm in our backs and his energy under my elbow.

A tear-stained Ada awaited us, comforting a weeping Ellie. They had all panicked to find me gone.

I have also said nothing to Thea of what was taking place between William and me at that time. In those days, people did not speak of what happens between husband and wife, and I prefer that it stays that way.

To say that we were estranged would be to put it too strongly. But we had lost each other. During our stay in Camberwell, I remembered every day what my mother said so long ago – that William was a white man, a soldier, and that he would vanish. It turned out not to be true. But now I saw there were more ways than just the physical in which a man might disappear. I recognised William might feel lost without the army, without the status and respect he enjoyed in Gibraltar, but he seemed too distant to reach, and I found no way to remedy this.

But it turned out that William was still his remarkable self. When I was in dry clothes beside the fire in the parlour, he said, 'I feel as if I lost you, my dear.'

'I was only taking a walk.'

'A somewhat impetuous and dangerous walk, my dear. In any case, that is not what I meant.' He placed his hand on his heart. 'I have lost you here. And I would like to find you again.'

I was so surprised, my mouth fell open. 'But I thought you were the one who was lost to me,' I say.

We talked then for the first time in many months. We talked of how William saw us as a team on the Rock – holding our separate roles in the society there and coming together at home as a family. I told him there were times when he vanished for me then – into his work.

'Like the time that big-big gun arrived.'

'The 100-ton gun, my dear.'

'Yes, that one. You fell in love with that gun.'

'And you, you fell in love – first with the Temperance Café, and then with Consuela. You used to talk to Consuela instead of me.'

'And now I have no Consuela. Let us not talk of her.'

'I never understood what went on between the two of you – at the end?'

'We fell out – over Dick and Almira. She sided with her sister. And spiteful, she turned spiteful, nuh. She was a sad widow. I suppose she was jealous of me.'

'So, you have no Consuela. And I have no guns. So I would like to fall back in love with my wife, but I find it's difficult when she is determined not to like my family. You disapprove of everything – my nieces, my brother, my job, even the weather. You used not to be like that.'

Such a remark made me indignant, and for a while we argued about almost everything, but particularly about the risk Henry and Charlotte were taking with their daughters' morals and how that might be affecting Ada with her new impertinent manner.

Then William spoke of his boyhood, when his younger brother Henry looked up to him, and their parents looked down on Henry because they favoured William. He told me how, in spite of this, Henry supported their parents at some considerable cost through their old age and illness, as well as giving a roof to Charlotte's widowed mother until she died, which I already knew. William reckoned he owed a great deal to his brother, who struggled to meet these responsibilities while we enjoyed the security of the army.

'Besides,' he added, 'it is true I lost my guns but, when I arrived in London, it was exhilarating to have no uniform, no Ps and Qs to watch, no commanding officer. I regret upsetting you, by drinking with Henry and so on. I'm sorry my job displeases you. But I intend to be successful in this new career. I am settled to it. I want to make a good new life, and I want us to embark upon it together. I would be glad to be a team again.'

Ah, William. You were a good man and a wise one. What could I do then but embrace you and promise to support you? I wish you were here now to give me encouragement.

Plymouth
Saturday 31st October 1931

Dear Thea,

You may remember in my last letter I was looking forward to going to chapel in Sheerness as a family. Ada and Ellie told me about the café run by Wesleyan ladies and that they had met the Reverend Payne and his wife there on occasion. But this did not prepare me for what happened at the end of service on Sunday morning. I was already a little discomfited. The Minister had taken as his text 'Judge not, that ye be not judged' and I was aware of William looking sideways at me. I was glad of the spirited singing of 'As with Gladness Men of Old' which concluded the service.

The Minister and his wife are standing by the door, greeting people as they leave. As we approach, Ada steps in front of William and me, shakes the Minister by the hand, and embraces his wife before turning to present us as we stand wide-eyed and uncertain behind her. They seem pleasant enough people, but it is inappropriate of Mrs Payne to give such careful attention to Ada.

'Oh, Mama,' says Ada, 'I did not mean to embarrass you. That is the last thing I wished to do. But I do not see how else I could have conducted myself, given my acquaintance with the Reverend and Mrs Payne. I hoped to be courteous in introducing my parents to them. In future, of course, I will always follow behind you.'

I am mollified, but it is not an apology. I decide to be gracious and not insist. These manners may seem old-fashioned to you now, Thea, in this modern day where folks behave so informally. But it was different then and I did not want a daughter of mine to appear unmannerly.

Afterwards, William surprises me by saying he is pleased at Ada showing more confidence and making her own way. At least he did not say that to Ada herself. But I tell him I expect more support when I see fit to reprimand the children. He never was so lax in Gibraltar. In fact, I often thought him harsh. Consuela and I would tease him for applying the rules of the military at home. I can only assume this to be the influence of his brother and his undisciplined family.

Consuela. She is still difficult to forget. Often in Camberwell, I heard her voice at my elbow, urging me to take more pleasure in my nieces and their activities. Sometimes, I believe I became more critical of them just to spite Consuela who, of course, knew nothing of my predicament. What a foolish and fanciful notion! It is not, however, fanciful to imagine that Consuela would delight in this new version of Ada, and would take her part against me and my principles. I remind myself firmly that, when it suited her, Consuela was quick to take refuge behind her family and their prejudice. Standing by your principles can be hard, Thea, but first you must be clear what those principles are.

Ada, meanwhile, is full of schemes and enterprises. There seems to be no stopping her. She makes cookies – using my recipe – to take to the café. I must have betrayed a little indignation in my expression for she exclaims, 'Oh, Mama! You don't mind, do you? I promised Alice because they are so delicious.'

'So now it's Alice? Is that Mrs Payne you refer to?'

'She is such a dear. We get on so well. Why do you not come with me? I'm sure you would like her, and it would be like the old days on Main Street.'

I do go, but the café is not as well run as my old haunt in Gibraltar, and I have no role. There is no mention of Temperance, and I find the atmosphere a little superficial. Now that we are settled, it is time for me to be more active for the cause. I say nothing of this intention to Ada.

Her next idea is to sweet-talk her father into buying a piano.

'I plan to take children for lessons. Just the early stages, to get them started. I can pay you back, Papa, with my earnings. Alice, Mrs Payne, that is, tells me there are several children at Sunday school who want to learn. Did I tell you she has asked me to teach at Sunday school?'

Indeed she had not mentioned it and, although I consider it an honour, I wish she had consulted me before accepting. I say as much to William, but he just laughs.

'She reminds me of you, my dear, at that age. Full of energy and enthusiasm.'

What am I to say?

Of course, William gives in and finds her a piano, which is installed in the parlour. Now I have to listen to her pupils' faltering notes and discords every afternoon when school is out.

William is much away with his work for the brewery, persuading the public houses of Kent to buy their ale. I take one such absence as the opportunity to visit the publican next door to us. I plan to speak to him on the subject of clearing our garden, but I also take a handful of Temperance leaflets with me. I go after Ellie is in bed, but early in the evening before the effects of too much liquor on the drinkers might make my visit unpleasant. Even so, my entrance is greeted with ribaldry, as the men are unused to seeing a lady in their domain. The landlord comes forward to greet me and asks what I will drink. He speaks in jest, and there is general laughter of a coarse kind, which I ignore, tackling my concern about our garden straight away.

He laughs in my face. 'I like a woman who's direct, and I'll be direct back to you, Mrs Silking. The answer is no. I need the storage, ma'am, and I have the right. 'Tis written in the lease.'

The reek of his breath is so strong that I fear it might make me tipsy. I start to protest, but he cuts rudely across me. 'Now, if you'll excuse me, I have some thirsty customers. By the way, ma'am, I find it curious that you come asking instead of your husband, and you choose to come when your husband is away on brewery business.'

There is a guffaw from the counter at this remark, but I refrain from looking round. The publican's opening the door to show me out, but I stand on my dignity, remembering my pamphlets. 'I will not detain you,' I say. 'I'll just distribute these before I leave.'

I'm shaking when I get back indoors, but Ada has finished the dishes and is practising at her piano. She hasn't noticed that I've been out.

I get severely rebuked by William for this incident. 'I hear you visited our neighbour and upset his customers by going from table to table haranguing them on the evils of drink. I understand your feelings, I really do. I know it is hard for you to live in these conditions, given your beliefs. But such behaviour risks our livelihood, the very roof over our heads.'

He steps close then to take my hand, which I'm reluctant to give. 'I thought we were to be a team,' he says. 'We have to work together.'

I have to promise my husband I will not repeat this behaviour, which is not hard. I never want to set foot in that evil establishment again. But I'm left wondering what William's half of the team was doing when he refused to raise the question of the garden with the publican.

There is a postscript to this story. Inevitably it involves Ada. She meets the publican's wife in the drapers. They get talking, and Ada discovers this woman's dearest wish is for her youngest child to learn piano. Ada strikes a bargain with her. The woman talks to her husband, the publican, and the payment for the music lessons comes in the shape of their eldest son digging our garden. The kegs are removed, and only one stack of crates remains, no doubt to maintain the terms of the lease and their right of access to our yard.

This result shows me two things: that there are always more ways than one to solve a problem, and that I must stop looking upon Ada as a child.

Your affectionate grandmother,
Henrietta Silking

Sheerness was all about Ada. Looking back, I can see that. She stepped out from behind me when I wasn't looking, just as she did that Sunday morning in chapel. Before I knew it, she was the one they referred to, looked up to. I was in her shadow.

I blamed that family of Henry and Charlotte's, of course. I underestimated the strength of Ada's affection for her cousins. I thought it superficial, like the girls themselves. Of course, Ada was not concerned when I instructed her not to keep replying to Minnie's letters. Because, all along, it was Violet she was most attached to. I saw no harm when she made a card for Violet's fourteenth birthday, since she was only a child. Little did I know what was to come.

I wonder about that forward streak I saw in Ada when we first arrived in Sheerness – if I had nipped it a little more firmly in the bud, would I have had a happier time in that town? For, as time went on, I saw Ada fulfilling roles that had once been mine. It was hard to see her so respected – carrying all before her with a grace and dignity she had learned from me. I am ashamed to admit that I saw her as the usurper of my rightful place. I was, I suppose, jealous of what I now see was the natural order of things. Her youth and energy, her "enlightened" attitudes, which I considered 'flighty', were merely taking over from a tired old woman. The woman who William saw as disapproving while he talked of Ada's "enterprise" and admired her new confidence.

Plymouth
Saturday 7th November 1931

Dear Thea,

Ada and her new-found confidence continued to worry me. At this distance, my worries do not seem so very big, especially viewed from the other side of war and death, but at the time they loomed large.

It is the summer of 1901. The country has survived the death of the old Queen, and Ada and I have regained the closeness we used to share in Gibraltar. In warm weather, we link arms and promenade along the pier, marvelling at how pleasant Sheerness can be when the wind from Siberia is not knifing through the thickest wraps to chill our bones. Ada seems to be calming down.

Earlier in the year, she alarmed me by setting up her easel by the shore and sitting half the day painting pictures of the estuary, the ships and the racing clouds. I tried to persuade Ellie to go with her, but for once Ellie was not biddable. She found the activity too dull. Ada would attract a knot of interested people, young men amongst them, who I feared were there to admire the painter as much as the painting. It did not seem suitable.

To my relief, Ada becomes friends with a girl from chapel. Louisa is rather a plain girl, but good-natured and sensible. I am reassured that Ada now has a companion of her own age in her activities around the town, and is therefore less likely to be the subject of gossip. For, believe me, people in a small town will gossip at the slightest departure from convention, and Ada departs frequently before she calms down.

Louisa owns a bicycle and persuades Alice Payne to loan Ada hers. For weeks, Ada drags Ellie and Louisa to the least frequented streets in town to support her in learning to ride. Ada wants no witnesses to her undignified progress and frequent tumbles. William, of course, is in favour of the venture, and I agree on condition that she wears her normal attire. I am shocked by the fashion amongst some lady cyclists of exchanging their skirts for bloomers. After that, the two girls take off on every pleasant day to ride into the Kentish countryside with a picnic in their baskets.

'Mama,' Ada says to me one day, 'you have no idea how wonderful it is to feel the wind inside one's petticoats, cooling your legs as you spin along!'

I do have some idea, and it gives me cause for concern. Would bloomers be more seemly, after all? Be that as it may, when Louisa's brother, Albert, suggests that he and a friend join the girls to cycle out for a picnic one Saturday, I refuse to allow it. I am remembering Ada's description of the horse galloping in the meadow. Those posters do not lie. England in summer is enchanting. Alice Payne teaches us new names for flowers every time we walk out together. The meadows are indeed enticing. Too enticing. No galloping amongst wild flowers will take place in the presence of young men if I have anything to do with it.

That year, it seems I am continually substituting a lesser evil to protect Ada from what I perceive to be a greater moral danger. So it is that, when Ada tells me that her cousin Violet is eager for her to visit Camberwell, I give in more readily than she expects. It will put some distance between her and this Albert. Also, Violet's sister, Nellie, has recently married a sergeant major in the Royal Artillery, so I am reassured that a steadying influence has joined the family.

Then, in the autumn, when Ada returns from Camberwell, comes the business of the pantomime. Evidently, it is Violet's idea. Ada is fired up with the idea of putting on Dick Whittington to raise funds for the Wesleyan Foreign Mission with which both Ada and I are closely involved. In spite of recognising the influence of Violet in this new enterprise, I welcome it. The play will be a decorous production suitable for family entertainment and bearing no resemblance to a music hall show. It will be for charity rather than commercial. But, best of all, Ada will be occupied in fund-raising for the Mission instead of applying to join them overseas.

We have been entertaining several delegations of missionaries from China, India and the Bahamas. I've noticed, with some concern on these occasions, that Ada constantly strays from serving tea to engage in deep discussion with the women amongst the group. Remembering my own long-ago desire to travel the world when I was a young girl, I understand how tempting it may be. I pray fervently that she will not be persuaded to travel to these far-flung and dangerous places, and fear that she will return to her obsession with China – her favoured destination – when the pantomime is over.

But, at that point, Albert is to step in, as you will see. This time, I consider him to be more of a rescuer than a threat. But I run ahead.

Mrs Payne and the ladies at chapel are much taken with the idea of the pantomime, a committee is formed, and Ada starts on the task of making a wardrobe and schooling the Sunday school children who will form the chorus of rats.

Ada and Louisa make a habit of meeting in the afternoons at the house of the Reverend and Mrs Payne to sew the costumes. It comes to my notice that Louisa's brother, Albert, begins to make a similar habit of calling there after work to walk the girls home. It is further reported to me that Louisa often finds herself detained by other errands, leaving Albert to escort Ada alone.

I call on Mrs Payne to protest about this arrangement. But the young woman is quite indignant.

'Do not think I am unaware of the proprieties,' says she. 'But what am I to do when they have once left my doorstep?'

'You could send Louisa with them instead of detaining her.'

'I assure you it is not I who detains her. But, Mrs Silking, do you not think Albert is a very admirable and hard-working young man? The Woodfords are a most respectable family. He and Ada seem so well suited.'

I refrain from telling Mrs Payne that it is no business of hers. Maybe she imagines she is rescuing Ada from a life 'on the shelf'. Mrs Payne is certainly no ally, in spite of being the Minister's wife. I am not surprised to see more than one secret smile exchanged between her and Louisa after service, when Albert starts to be a regular chapelgoer.

The pantomime is a great success. Ada is acclaimed for her skill in producing it and is much in the limelight, receiving bouquets at the end of the final performance. No mention is made of the small part of kitchen maid in which she made the mistake of casting herself. Albert attends all three showings, and applauds until he nearly falls off his seat.

Your affectionate grandmother,
Henrietta Silking

I screw the top on my pen and stretch my hand which aches from writing so much. My head aches, too, from the memories. So much worry about such minor things, as it turned out.

Now, in Plymouth, as darkness falls, the neighbourhood begins to pop and fizz with fireworks, which mushroom into rainbow stars in the night sky, a pleasure to the eye. The young lads have been up and down the street all week with their effigies in old prams, asking for 'a penny for the guy'. Some people had their Guy Fawkes display on Thursday, but today is favoured by husbands who have had the afternoon to prepare. Ada told me they have promised young John a display, so he and his parents are staying on after tea and catching the late bus.

I cannot resist going to the landing window. From there, I can see the dark shape of Albert, vigorous and stocky, and of Cyril, tall and hesitant, moving about in the garden. I hope they are managing to cooperate with no harsh words to spoil the atmosphere. Ada will have poked chestnuts into the embers of the living room fire, and she and John will be exclaiming as they struggle to hold them and peel them while they're still hot. John will be eager to rush outside to position a rocket with his father, but he will be obliged to watch behind the safety of the window. I trust

Ada will have given him the packet of sparklers I purchased from the newsagent. I smile to think of him running round the room waving the spluttery stick and frightening his mother with the sparks that fly. Ada will have passed them off as a gift from herself. Otherwise, the silly woman might forbid him to enjoy them.

Plymouth
Saturday 14th November 1931

Dear Thea,

Today, I think to cheer myself on a grey November day with happy memories. In case you think I lost control of my daughter, Ada, and that she was to become a wayward girl, I tell you, she did find a good and steady man to marry in that bleak town.

After the pantomime, Albert and Ada begin openly courting. I begin to see that for all her exuberance and impulsiveness, Ada has learned more of my restraining wisdom than I realised. I have also taught her that a woman can be strong and independent, so how can I blame her for her initiative? Now, she is learning to channel her energy, and to take the balanced view that a woman, however strong, is better off with a reliable husband.

It is unfortunate that, when Ada marries, we add another Albert to the family confusion, but I can hardly ask him to change his name. Albert and his family are well respected in the town, both father and son being skilled workers in the shipbuilding industry, so his future employment is assured.

I look back on 1905 as a very happy year, when the Lord blessed Ada and Albert with a baby boy. The young married couple were living with us in Ada's old room. But when Ada announced she was with child, it was suggested that they might not wish to bring up a child next door to a public house. Albert's parents had a room becoming free when their lodger left, so they could move in there. I believe it was a clever ruse of Albert's mother to make sure she saw more of her grandchild.

Fortunately, I was able to save a little face – because William was retiring a few months before Ada's expected confinement. As our house belonged to the brewery, we would be obliged to move, probably to a smaller, more manageable property. I told Albert's mother that, regrettably, we would no longer have room for them. I was a little sad to see them go, but it was a sadness tinged with relief. I still find Albert a difficult man, and he was no easier in those early days, in spite of his worship of Ada. He had very strong opinions, which William did not share. As to seeing Cyril, as soon as the baby was old enough, Ada called in most days and often left him with me while she did her shopping, so I had no reason to complain.

Shortly after Cyril's arrival, we hear the good news that Henry, our eldest boy, has obtained his commission, meaning that he is now Lieutenant Silking. William finds himself a very proud father on top of being a grandfather, and makes an unfortunate visit to the public house, even though we no longer live next door. What can I do but nurse him and forgive him and tell the family he has a fever? No man is perfect.

More happiness was to follow when Dick and Bertie both got home postings, Dick from Gibraltar and Bertie from South Africa, while Ernest was stationed at Woolwich after returning from Bermuda. You can imagine we had some lively weekends with the boys visiting, sleeping on the couch and on the floor in the little house in Wood Street, and finding out how it was to be an uncle.

Your affectionate grandmother,
Henrietta Silking

As I finish this letter, it occurs to me that the letters about the happy times turn out to be the shorter ones I write. How this year of 1931 contrasts with 1905, when I sat proudly at table with my family around me. Since then, three of them have been taken by the good Lord, but I will not dwell upon that today.

Strangely, the image that sticks in my mind is of Ada as scullery maid in that pantomime which I described in last week's letter. It was a filler interlude to allow people to move scenery and change costumes backstage. Dick Whittington had run away, and there stood the maid in front of the curtain, with her mop and bucket, wringing her hands and weeping for the loss of Dick, her only friend in the world. It was immediately apparent that, for all the coaching she might have received from her talented cousins, Ada was no actress. Try as she might to look grief-stricken, the "tears" were unconvincing and the twist of her mouth made her look confused and embarrassed, which mirrored the feelings of the audience. Thankfully, it was a brief scene.

So why does it revisit me so powerfully today? I stretch my old limbs and creak my way down to the kitchen to make myself a pot of tea to help me work it out.

But it doesn't come to me until I wake at two o'clock the following morning, as I often do. The truth strikes me hard. I have seen a similar display of grief on Ada much more recently – right here in my kitchen – when she came to tell me that I was no longer welcome at tea on Saturdays. I see I have been doing a good job deceiving myself all this time.

'It is not her fault'. Not Ada's fault. That's what I told the boy, John, in my letter, the first letter I wrote. I didn't want him to think ill of Ada, his adoring grandmother. But I was also trying to fool myself.

I did not believe in Ada's tears, even then. Her story had no ring of truth. She said it was Edith insisting that John never sees me. The idea that Cyril's wife would lay down the law to her mother-in-law about who she has to tea – it makes no sense. Ada is a powerful woman; she likes to be in charge, nuh. That story of hers makes me grunt in disbelief. Ada was keen to lay the blame somewhere outside the family. On the edge, at least. She's not as good an actress as she thinks. I know that girl inside out. But I buried that knowing deep down inside me.

Now I see that I didn't believe in her distress any more than I believed in that scullery maid.

I have been fighting not to admit this to myself. I'm still fighting not to examine the implications.

Plymouth
Saturday 9th April 1932

Dear Thea,

Such a long time has elapsed since I wrote to you. I have been gravely ill with pneumonia. I lost Christmas and most of January while poor Ada nursed me. She had to sleep beside me for fear of a crisis, and the doctor visited daily during the worst week, although I remember nothing of it. It has been a slow convalescence, with Ada bringing me food and watching to be sure I eat a little. It is only since the daffodils began to blossom that I have ventured out, and this is the first week I feel strong enough to lift a pen.

When I wrote of Ada's "turbulent year", it was nothing compared with what emerged later.

William has not been long retired, and it is just after Cyril's second birthday when grave news reaches us from Camberwell. A postcard comes with a scrawl from Henry. Violet is in the hospital, knocked unconscious in a fall. William is immediately of a mind to go to London, but I tell him there will be nothing he can do except waste his pension on the train fare.

Of course, when Ada comes round with Cyril, it's the first thing I tell her. She claps her hand over her mouth and blushes dark red.

'So that is why I've not heard from her!' It blurts out of her before she can stop it.

'You were actually expecting to hear from her?' I ask. 'What did you expect to hear?'

But then the girl clams up. She brushes it off as nothing particular. But I see she is preoccupied, worried beyond a natural concern for her cousin's condition.

A few days later, we get a proper letter. William's brother writes that Violet is out of danger. She regained consciousness and is at home, although she has her broken arm set in a plaster cast.

Of course, my first thought is that she fell when prancing about on the stage. Aloud I say, 'How did it all happen? Did she fall downstairs?'

William looks up from reading the letter. 'She was on one

of these damn fool marches, demanding votes for women. Suffragettes, they're calling them. Violet got knocked over in the crowd, it seems. She was lucky not to be arrested. They're putting them in prison, you know.'

I say nothing to William, but I'm convinced Ada is somehow involved.

When I question her, Ada is clearly upset, and eventually the whole story comes out. Just a few weeks before, Violet wrote to Ada asking if she was willing to donate money to 'the cause'.

'She said she knew I couldn't march, because of having Cyril, but she thought I'd want to help in another way.'

'But you didn't…?'

She lifts her head, a gesture of defiance I haven't seen in Ada for some years. 'Yes, I did. It's important. Women—'

'You sent money? Albert's hard-earned money? Does Albert know?'

She looks shamefaced then. 'It was my money. I took it from my savings. But I didn't dare tell him. No, Mama, before you say it, I know it is no way to carry on.'

'And I think you know what else I'm about to say.'

'Just don't start talking about the monkey climbing too high. You think it serves poor Violet right, but she will think it worth it. It's a scandal that women are not allowed to vote. I'd have thought you would be all for it. It fits with Wesleyan principles, you know it does.'

'I'm well aware of that. The great John Wesley himself considered women of equal stature to men in God's eyes. He held them in high esteem.'

Ada sighs. 'Do you not think, Mama, that we should also be equal in the eyes of the world?'

I have to agree. 'Of course. And the world would benefit. It's not the principle of the vote I'm against, only the campaign of violence. The ends do not justify the means, in my opinion.'

'It is regrettable—'

'The other thing I say, Ada, it is a scandal that you keep this from your husband. You may have secrets from your mother, but don't have them from Albert, or he will learn not to trust you.'

'I know, Mama, I know. I've been foolish.' She breaks into tears and I am pleased to comfort her, as well as little Cyril who wakes from his nap at that moment.

The incident becomes the subject of an uncomfortable discussion at lunch on Sunday. The question of whether women should be allowed to vote turns out to be the first issue worthy of strong opinions that William and Albert agree upon.

Poor Albert turns on Ada, looking bemused, hurt even. 'How long have you been harbouring these beliefs? Your cousin Violet must have known you were sympathetic.'

It turns out that when Ada went to stay in Camberwell, she got involved with both Nellie and Violet in distributing pamphlets about this vote for women. That was nearly five years ago. All that time, Violet has persisted in her support for the madness.

'You knew nothing of this subversive activity?' Albert looks to William to answer the question.

William shakes his head in disbelief. 'She never mentioned it.'

'And Violet's parents, did they not intervene?'

'Evidently not,' says William, unable to conceal his discomfort.

By this time, I know from Henry's letters that both he and Charlotte support the movement, but William and I have agreed not to divulge this fact. They did discourage Violet from attending the march, but only on account of the weather being so bad. Apparently, the press of people was so great that Violet was unable to keep her footing in the mud. It was fortunate she was not trampled to death. All week, I have had the gravest difficulty in not saying 'I told you so.'

Albert is speaking again, looking from William to Ada and back again. 'You do know what these women are about, don't you? Firing churches? Smashing shop windows? They stop at nothing. They are dangerous!'

I see from Ada's expression that this news has not reached her ears. 'I would not be part of such activity,' she says, looking shocked.

I can also see that Albert is thinking that he might not have been so keen to propose marriage to Ada had he known of her involvement when they were stepping out. Most of the time he sets the girl on a pedestal, but, just now, he is struggling to keep her there. And Ada is not helping him in this endeavour. She shows not contrition but great indignation, and instead of having the wisdom to fall silent continues to argue the cause for women having the vote.

Dick turns out to be the only one to support Ada. He is home for the weekend, being stationed in Shoeburyness. He speaks in his usual thoughtful way. 'Of course, not all women are fit to influence the running of the country. But many men are not, and that includes many who find themselves in that position in Parliament. I would back a sensible woman against one of those any day. Our own mother is a fine example of such a capable woman, wouldn't you say?'

Dick looks from William to Albert, who find themselves unable to riposte. If they disagree, William will seem to betray his wife and Albert to insult his mother-in-law.

Albert turns instead to Ada and says quietly, 'I am sure you acted with the enthusiasm of youth, encouraged by your wayward cousin. But now you have a family to care for, I trust you will put these matters behind you?'

I hold my breath, waiting for Ada's response.

She swallows hard and looks upon the floor as she speaks. 'Of course, I put my child first at all times. That is why I did not march. Besides, I would not travel to London without consulting you.' At last, she raises her eyes to meet Albert's gaze. 'You can trust me to know where my duty lies.'

At this point, I stand to put a full stop to the discussion, indicating to Ellie that she should clear the table.

While Ada and Ellie take care of the dishes in the scullery, Dick and Albert stand out under the front porch for a smoke. As I tidy up, I get the drift of their conversation from odd words that float in through the letterbox. First, Dick is feigning a sudden interest in the latest shipbuilding methods. Then he inquires whether Ada's still teaching in Sunday school. He is bent on restoring Albert's pride and on helping him to put Ada back on her pedestal. I trust she will not insist on jumping from it in the future.

It pains me to know that all the time I was concerned at the trivial "wildness" that took hold of Ada before she met Albert, there were more serious issues afoot that I knew nothing of. But, as you will learn, that is the nature of motherhood when children grow to independence and keep secrets.

Your affectionate grandmother,
Henrietta Silking

Even the suffragette business was not so serious, when I think back. It turned out those women were not foolish after all. If I am honest, if I had been in Ada's shoes as a young woman, I would probably have been a supporter.

Those nieces of William's weren't bad girls, either. They were clearly professional in what they did. There were no more trips to New York, but William told me they were appearing on billboards all over the pantomime circuit in the north of England – Bradford and Leeds – not to mention Aberdeen and Glasgow in Scotland. I noticed Albert's eyes light up one time when Ada mentioned them. Evidently, he'd heard of the Sisters Silking. Maybe he hoped for tickets. I was told they sang with spirit – which I can believe – and danced very gracefully, even if it was pantomime in the burlesque style and no doubt full of lewd innuendo. Ada assured me they never dressed as men. The very idea.

But I'm an old woman now. This letter has exhausted my strength and I feel the need to take myself straight to my bed.

Plymouth
Saturday 16th April 1932

Dear Thea,

I must try to make this a short letter, the last one was too much, and I was obliged to stay in my bed the following day, feeling too weak even to attend chapel.

After the business with the suffragettes, things calm down. For one thing, Violet marries, not unfortunately a sensible soldier but another artiste in the music hall. I am surprised to hear from Ada that she's continuing on the stage, but it does mean she's ceased her involvement in the campaign. At least she has a husband to keep his eye on her, and maybe she'll begin to think of babies instead of votes.

Next comes the marriage of my son, Bertie, followed by a steady stream of babies. Their household in Brabourne makes the arrangements of Henry and Charlotte in Camberwell seem a model of organisation. The main thing is they are happy, but I do not see eye to eye with Bertie's wife. Ada and Ellie visit frequently, but I tell them that William and I are too old to travel, which is not the case at all.

It turns out, I speak too soon. William is taken from me later that year, in the summer of 1909.

It is a warm evening in August, and we take a stroll on the pier. We chat to friends and sit a while on a bench, watching the sea birds and admiring the light on the water, which is unusually still. We return in good spirits and William sits in his chair while I prepare a light repast. I call him when it's ready, but get no response.

I call again. 'William! You are becoming so deaf, these days.'

Still no answer.

Impatient, I put my head round the parlour door. His head is slumped forward onto his chest.

'You've not fallen asleep already? Oh, William, come!'

Still nothing. A sudden fear grips me. I run forward and take his head in my hands. It is heavy, and he makes no attempt to lift it. I shake him, feel for his pulse, and lay my ear against his chest. His heart has stopped. That steady beating, which has lulled me to sleep, night after night, year after year, is silent.

I cry out so loudly that the neighbours hear my lamentations and come to the door. The good woman sits with me while her son runs to fetch the doctor and then to Ada's house on the other side of town.

Ada is distraught by her father's passing. She and William were so close, and he always championed her. But Albert turns out to be a pillar of strength. He makes all the necessary practical arrangements and pays out of his own pocket without a word, before it becomes clear that William subscribed to a club for the purpose.

I am pleased to discover that William left me by no means destitute. Not that there was ever a threat of the workhouse. Neither the family nor the folk at chapel would have seen me reduced to that. Besides, Ellie is bringing in a small wage from her work at the library. While I wait for the lawyers to release the money, I'm able to dip into the shoebox at the back of the wardrobe where my secret nest egg has been slowly accumulating over the years.

The Reverend and Mrs Payne are long gone, of course, and I've struck up a friendship with Mrs Gilpin, the current Minister's wife. She brings me great comfort over the following months. Eventually, there comes a time when Ellie and I no longer weep into our cocoa of an evening, when I no longer lie awake all night, nor wake in a startle to find myself alone in the bed. Instead, I find myself overtaken by inexplicable anger. At least it gives me back my energy. After Ellie leaves in the morning, I set to, scrubbing and sweeping with vigour, and all the time yelling at William, accusing him of abandoning me.

'Now was the time to enjoy some leisure,' I tell him. 'To have some pleasure in life, and you go and leave me all alone!'

I cry hot tears of rage instead of the cold weeping of sadness as before.

Before I have time to emerge from this madness, another disruption arrives. For some time, Ada's Albert has been keen to progress his career but has found no opportunity in the Sheerness yard. Ada arrives on my doorstep full of concern and suppressed excitement. Albert has heard from my son, Henry, who is stationed in the Plymouth garrison, that good opportunities exist in Devonport Dockyard. Albert has taken steps and secured a good position with prospects. They are to move to Devon. Ada doesn't want to leave me behind. She suggests that Ellie and I accompany them and we make savings by combining our households.

Meanwhile, Ada and my boys club together to put up a proper memorial to their father. When it is erected, we all go to the cemetery to lay flowers. It stands out from the neighbouring graves for its size, and I'm pleased with the simple design of a plain but imposing cross. The inscription gives his rank, so his professional status is recorded. He would like that. It grieves me that I'm to stay so short a time in Sheerness and so will be unable to tend the grave. I will plant some daffodil bulbs and instruct young Bertie to look after the weeding of it. But with his family's harum-scarum ways, I wonder if he will remember.

Your affectionate grandmother,
Henrietta Silking

Yes, that was a fine memorial we put up to my William. I hope Bertie has kept it tidy. I only wish I had a photograph of it. But, what does it matter? He is with the good Lord and he lives on in my heart.

Dear Thea,

Devonport turns out not to be a desirable place to live. I never thought I would say this, but Sheerness seems pleasant and genteel in comparison. There are too many public houses and too many sailors. Not a good combination. The street where we live is, thankfully, not so run-down as some and has no tavern, and our little house is pleasant enough. Most of the residents here are respectable working people. But you do not have to walk far to find a neighbourhood it is best not to enter. There are streets in the vicinity where certain ladies, who are not ladies, are known to work, and which contain sights you would not want a six-year-old to see.

Cyril gets bullied at school and is so frequently ill that he learns more from his mother than from the teachers. The location is, of course, convenient for Albert's work, but before long Ada starts to work hard at persuading him to move to a better area, if only for their son's sake. But Albert tends to caution, and Ada cannot prevail upon him to take on a higher rent until his position is more secure and he sees what prospects the future might bring. I offer to teach Cyril myself. After all, I'm qualified to do so. But Ada maintains that he needs to mix with other children.

Eventually, Albert agrees to pay for Cyril to attend what used to be called a 'dame school', run by a Miss Prettyjohn in her front room. She takes six children who call her 'Miss John', because, as she says, 'I am not at all pretty,' which cleverly deals with the odd name. Miss Prettyjohn has a dog, a shaggy mongrel called Tinker, that she claims does most of the teaching.

Certainly, taking Tinker for regular history and geography walks is a large part of the curriculum. Cyril tells us he can only do algebra with a dog at his feet, but Albert steadfastly refuses to replicate that situation at home. For once, I find myself in agreement with my son-in-law. But I'm glad to see Cyril coming home with a smile on his face.

Soon we receive more happy news. Dick writes to say he's getting married at the ripe old age of forty. He left the army at the end of his second period of service and found work in the dockyard in Portsmouth. His intended is the landlady where he lodges, a widow lady with two little girls.

This lady is, of course, your mother, Thea!

Next thing, my Henry visits with more news. Not to be outdone by his younger brother, he too is marrying at the even riper age of forty-five. Another widow lady, but with no little girls. She is Welsh, and they marry in Pembroke so we do not attend the wedding. But I'm happy that they settle not far from us, in Mutley.

Dick plans a quiet wedding and tells us not to spend the money travelling to it. Instead, he will meet up with us on their honeymoon. He has booked a week in a small boarding house in Torpoint as a surprise for his bride. So, one day we all take the ferry across the Tamar, including Henry and his new wife, Agnes. We meet up with Dick and Flo and catch the motor charabanc to Whitsand Bay. What an excitement!

I take to your mother, Flo, at once – a sensible woman who evidently brought up her own sister and brother when their mother was taken from them when she was only twelve years old. But, of course, you know that, Thea. What a happy day we spend, picnicking on the sands and gazing across sparkling water to the far horizon. Henry and Dick go swimming, racing to be first in the sea. When I tell them to take care, Henry teases me.

'We know! "The sea ain't got no back door."' Henry's always been such a mimic, and everyone laughs at how he copies my accent. For, it is true, I fall into the language of my childhood when I quote those old proverbs. I notice Agnes doesn't find it so funny when he mimics her Welsh lilt. Albert declines to join the swimmers, but Ada persuades him to go paddling with Cyril. The sun shines, and we return home a tired and happy crew.

You were born two years later, and I rejoiced that Dick would know the joys of fatherhood. Little did we know then that war was just around the corner. Ernest re-enlisted at once, and both he and Bertie were sent to France, so anxious years followed. Your father wasn't fit and was in a reserved occupation in the dockyard, so I did not have to worry about him.

I was approaching seventy-five before we moved to a better area. I was now entitled to a small pension, which contributed to the rent. The war was over, and both Ernest and Bertie had survived the fighting in France. Ellie worked as a clerk in the dockyard, Henry was living nearby and I was pleased to have made your acquaintance, Thea! I was able to rest a little. During the war, Ada worked as a VAD, so I took responsibility for Cyril when he came home from school. Now, he needed no such supervision, but he still liked to talk to me, and it was good to feel wanted.

Ada has a rose – she spends a lot of time tending her roses – which is a favourite because it blooms not only in June along with all the others but again in September. I forget the name of it. But I think I resembled that autumn-flowering rose at that time. I was seventy-five years old, I was content, and I'd come to terms with losing my William. I still talked to him every day – and I found he agreed with me more often than he did in life.

I look now at the photograph Albert took of me that summer and I see someone at peace. My boys had been spared and were settled, and I saw my girls every day. I was content.

How lucky was that woman in the picture, living in a kind of idyll. Little did she know. 'Trouble don't set up like rain,' which is to say you can't always see it coming.

Your affectionate grandmother,
Henrietta Silking

Ada is lucky with her Albert. He is a difficult man, stubborn and dictatorial, but he does worship Ada. Once I was dusting their bedroom in the house in Garfield Terrace, and I found a valentine card where he'd written: 'To all the world but one. To me, all the world.' I'm sure, in private, he would write the same thing today, but nobody would guess it from the way he behaves.

I treasure the memory of our day at the beach. It belongs to a golden age, before the sadness came upon us. At the time, it put me in mind of our grand picnic in Gibraltar, but when I said as much to Dick, his face clouded over and he said he didn't recall much about it. I suppose it reminded him of Almira and was surprised how much that still affected him. But I didn't want to mention that to Thea.

To change the subject, I said, 'Flo seems a good woman, but I would have liked to meet her before you were wed.'

'This time, Mother, I wanted no interference. And yes, Flo–'

'Interference? Not from me, I hope.'

'You meant well, I know that. Back in Gib. Visiting Almira's mother–'

'I was only trying to help…'

He gave a great sigh. 'I know. But, as it happened, it didn't help. Quite the reverse. People always think they need to fight my battles for me.' He spoke softly, to himself almost. Certainly not to me. 'Let's not stir it all up. Least said, soonest mended. But with Flo, I wanted it to be just her and me.'

I didn't let it put a blight on the day. Sometimes, Dick misses the point. On the way back to the charabanc, he put his arm around me, as if to cancel out what he had said.

Plymouth
Saturday 21st May 1932

Dear Thea,

No mother should have to bury their child. Your mother, Thea, has suffered this, and I feel for her. Her child was but a few days old, not yet a personality. The children whom the Lord took from me were full-grown adults, each dear to me in a unique and special way.

For, in the space of five years, I lost three of them. Henry was taken first – in the military hospital here in Devonport. They tell me he had cancer of the liver. His wife seemed to grieve more about the delay in obtaining the pension than about losing her husband. I never did take to her.

Next came my brave soldier, Ernest, who signed up once again so eagerly in 1914, always quick to support a cause against injustice. He survived the war, and was demobbed in 1920, but he was affected by what he saw, the comrades he lost. Or so Ada told me. She saw him once or twice when she travelled to visit Violet in Camberwell. He was living and working in Woolwich. Ada attended the inquest, and she assured me it was natural causes, a heart attack, like William. But I always felt there was something she was keeping from me, to spare my feelings. Knowing Ernest, maybe his fist somehow got involved. It certainly was no life for him, working as a labourer, still single and living in a working men's hostel.

Ernest was never very clever, but 'every fool got he sense', and with Ernest it was a sense of injustice. In civilian life, it got him in trouble, even when it was a matter of defending his own brother. But, in battle, according to Dick, he was a valued soldier. Evidently, Dick spoke to comrades of his who spoke of his courage and loyalty. He would risk his life to save an injured comrade and bring him back behind the lines to be treated. But because he also got in trouble, he wasn't given promotion or recognition. My dear hothead of a son.

I lost Ellie twice. And, to be honest, this is the loss that affected me most. My loyal, lovely girl lost her heart to a soldier, Gustav, a decent enough young man, but a young man who was convinced that there was no future in England after the war. He persuaded her to emigrate to Canada. He went ahead and found himself a job as a shoemaker somewhere in Ontario. Evidently, this was the trade he'd learned before he was conscripted in 1916, a solid kind of occupation which will always be in demand. As soon as Ellie heard he had work and a place for them to live, she was determined to join him and marry him.

I shall never forget the day she left. She clung to me and Ada and didn't know how to detach herself to board the train for Liverpool where she was to embark. I prayed she would have a smooth crossing and gave her a bundle of herbs to help her. We waved until she was out of sight, and couldn't stop from weeping every time we thought of her for days after. So that was the first time I lost her.

Ellie married her sweetheart as soon as she arrived in Ontario. She sent us a photograph of the pair of them, and they looked so lost and alone. She wrote of all the strange things she found in this new country and of the rooms she was living in and how she was fixing it up to feel like home. Every time a letter came, we'd sit together in the kitchen, Ada and me, and Ada would read it aloud. Ellie had been married just over a year when she wrote that she'd fallen pregnant. I felt both joyful and sad that I would never see this grandchild. I would never see my Ellie as a mother. She wrote frequently about the progress of her pregnancy, how well she felt, how she was convinced it was a girl, but that Gustav hoped for a boy. She told us she would baptise a daughter Ada Henrietta, or Frederick Henry if a boy.

So imagine our distress when a letter from Gustav arrived, not announcing the arrival of the child, but telling us the baby was lost and Ellie gravely ill. It seemed she had the milk fever and was already taken from us by the time the first letter arrived, so long it took for the post to cross the ocean. So that was how I lost my Ellie a second time. Being at such a distance, I was hardly able to truly believe it.

'Yea, though I walk through the Valley of the Shadow of Death, I will fear no evil: for thou art with me.'

I found myself repeating this psalm over and over to myself. I found it a comfort after Henry died. It reassured me when Ernest was taken, but when the Lord saw fit to take Ellie, I confess I lost my faith.

'Blessed are they that mourn: for they shall be comforted.' That's what Ada kept repeating in those days. But I was not comforted then, and I am not comforted now.

Ada was shocked when I would not attend chapel. The Minister came to the house, but it was fully a year before I made my peace with the Lord.

I sincerely hope that you, Thea, never have to experience such pain.

Your affectionate grandmother,
Henrietta Silking

A mother should not have favourites. But I did. Of the boys, it was Dick. Of the girls, it was Ellie. Although, of course, circumstances have brought me closer to Ada. Writing of Ellie upsets me. Partly because I lost a beloved daughter. But also because it reminds me that there is something unspoken between me and my other daughter. That troubles me. It troubles me because it signifies that there is something about myself that I have not recognised. And it troubles me because Ada does not have the courage to tell me.

Only one person would have that courage. Consuela. Once again, I find myself wishing she would walk through the door. Maybe she wasn't being spiteful back then in Gibraltar. Maybe she really was acting out of friendship.

Plymouth
Saturday 13th April 1935

Dear Thea,

I thought I had finished with writing letters, but this one demands my attention.

I need to be straight with you before I die. By the time you receive these letters – if indeed you do receive them – you will know that you were prevented from reading them when I wrote them.

I believe that is on account of my West Indian origins and the colour of my skin.

The reason we did not see each other after our drive in the carriage when you were five years old had nothing to do with the distance between Portsmouth and Plymouth, which is what I wrote in my first letter. No. It was because of what your mother wrote to Ada. She told her what happened after that visit. She said all the people in the street contrived to have a peek at me. Then they understood why you looked the way you did then – a beautiful Caribbean child with lively hair and caramel skin good enough to eat. But they didn't see it that way. Instead, they saw fit to bully you at school, and even the teacher joined in. I'm sure your mother did not write of this to keep me away, but I deemed it unfair to inflict another visit on my relatives when it brought so much pain.

I hope you understand.

The next thing happened after I sent you that photograph. Your mother wrote to me. Reading between the lines of her letter, you were pretending to be a white person. She said you thought of yourself as a white person, that you had made yourself into a white person. This was the reason your mother gave for not giving you my letter. She did not want me to draw your attention to your origins. I have no way of knowing whether it is true that you consider yourself white – then or now. But I understand why you might want to do that, given the attitudes which prevail. Maybe you think it's the only way to get on in the world. It was clear to me when you were only five years old that you would want to do that. There is nothing wrong with such ambition. But be clear that you are not, and can never be, a white person. Whatever you achieve, and however well you convince others, at least do not be fooling yourself.

Here in Plymouth, my grandson's wife shares your mother's views. Since he was five years old, she did not want their little boy to know me. So I was no longer welcome when they visited my daughter on a Saturday afternoon. History repeats itself. Here am I, seventy years on, in the self-same position as my grandma – too black to sit at table with my grandson's family. And too black to write to my own granddaughter. How is the world to get rid of such prejudice if future generations do not understand their origins?

These days, I am very frail. I get breathless, as if I walk a mile between the kitchen and the living room. Often, I must force myself to rise of a morning. So, now I'm very tired from giving you a lecture you do not want to hear, but I need you to understand why you have not heard from me, and that I'm very upset not to be a proper grandmother to you.

From your affectionate grandmother,
Henrietta Silking

I had a dream that night.

I am on board a ship, which steams steadily across a vast ocean. As we approach land, I am standing on the deck, and the air is like a warm bath. The hot tap is running, and I feel the heat creeping up my limbs like a warm hug, relaxing my muscles and penetrating my bones.

Still in my dream, I think how cold I've been in England all the years. It's as if I know I'm dreaming, but I stay in the dream.

The heat brings perfumes with it, smells I haven't snuffed up for half a century. I breathe them in as I wait to disembark.

People start to move down the gangplank, waving at folk who are there to meet them. I look about but see no one I know. Then, a grey-haired woman right below me starts to beam up at me. She raises both her arms and I float down from the deck into her embrace. I have come home to my island, to my mama.

Maybe this dream is an omen. Maybe my time is near. I will bake my special cookies for Ada's next visit. I will ask her what it is that has come between us.

A knock at the door next Tuesday morning brings the answer to my question from a most unexpected visitor. Cyril's wife, that Edith, stands before me in one of her unfortunate hats.

'I hope I do not disturb you,' she says. 'I come at a time when I knew Ada would be out.' She looks anxiously down the road and I invite her to step inside.

It is indeed Ada's morning to go to town. We take a seat in the sitting room, more for my comfort than because I want to welcome her.

'I came because I saw you in the garden two Saturdays ago. This Saturday, at my request, Cyril did promise to have a word with his mother about that.'

I draw myself up. Am I now to be told I cannot appear in my own garden? But, as so often, I am too quick to judge.

'Cyril went into the kitchen, but lost his nerve, afraid

his father would overhear. He becomes another man in that house, in his father's presence.'

I nod, knowing this only too well. Cyril was always cowed by him, although Albert never laid a finger on him to my knowledge.

'So I decided to come and ask you myself.'

'Ask me what, Edith?'

I must sound fierce. She frowns, twisting the gloves she holds in her lap.

'I don't want to upset you. But you see, Ada told us that you were unable to walk. That was the reason she gave us some years back, when you didn't come to tea any more. Little John missed you, you see.'

'He did?' My eyes well up. 'Oh, Ada.'

'I thought at first when you didn't come that I had offended you. I wasn't receptive to your advice. I apologise. I...'

I hold up a hand. 'I'm always too free with advice. It was none of my business.'

'I was young and you had experience, but... Anyway, not long ago we thought to walk up the road to see you. Ada implied you were virtually bedridden. We didn't want to disturb. The next week I saw you - doing a bit of weeding.'

I brush my tears away. 'Tell me about young John. But first, I make us a cup of tea.'

'No, no. That is so kind, but I mustn't stay. If Ada were to...'

'Maybe we should invite her to join us?'

Edith's eyes widen in alarm. 'Oh, no. please don't tell

her I came. I wouldn't want to cause trouble between my Cyril and his mother. They think the world of each other.'

I watch her pull an envelope from her bag.

'I brought a photograph. Last summer. We were walking on the Hoe.' Her eyes light up with pride. 'He's doing well at school. He gets up to mischief, but he's a good boy.'

'I shall treasure it.' To reassure her fleeting frown I add, 'I'll keep it in my desk drawer.'

She pulls on her gloves. She's suddenly flustered and unsure.

I take her hand. 'Thank you, Edith. Thank you for coming.'

I watch her fasten the gate and hurry up the road to the bus stop. How I have misjudged that young woman in my mind. All because of Ada.

> Plymouth
> Wednesday 1st May 1935

Dear Ada

I cannot say how hard it is to be ashamed of the daughter who has been such a close and delightful companion for so many years. I trusted you and find myself betrayed.

Must I be ashamed because it was you who decided that little John should not know me?

Or must I be ashamed that you would not stand up to your husband (who adores you and will do whatever you say) because he considered that my presence would jeopardise the future of his grandson?

I was a fool to believe your tears when you told me not to

come on Saturdays – when you blamed it on poor Edith.

Later, some part of me recognised them as crocodile tears. But I was a coward and put it out of my mind.

I am still a coward because I have not confronted you since Edith revealed the truth of it. I could not bring myself to end my life in conflict with my dear daughter. Yes, Edith. She visited me because she saw me in the garden – which did not match your story that I was bedridden.

I suppose the dignified thing would be to keep quiet beyond the grave – but an anger and indignation rises up within me when I think of the many people of my colour who are treated badly – not in a small way within the family as I am – but with public humiliation and suffering. So I write to give you food for reflection on your behaviour and its consequences. I pray to the good Lord to forgive you. Consider it my dying wish that you make amends. Maybe you can find a way to smooth the way for Dick's daughter, Thea.

Yours still affectionately,

Your loving mother,

Henrietta Silking

Epilogue

There is no way of knowing whether John and Thea ever received Henrietta's letters.

Ada would have found them on her mother's death when her grandson, John, would have been ten years old. Ada would have wanted to avoid any upset to John and his progress into a successful future. She might have opened John's letter, or not. She might have kept it herself. Or she might have entrusted it to her son, Cyril, to do as he thought fit. Who knows?

Ada knew very little of Thea as an adult. So, it is likely that she sent the letters to her brother, Dick, to pass on to his daughter. Dick would have received them during the difficult years of Thea's first marriage. Relations between the families were strained, and Dick would have been concerned for Thea. There followed the deterioration of Dick's health and the outbreak of WWII. It is conceivable that Dick never found a good time to give Thea those letters.

When Portsmouth was bombed, Dick and Flo moved to Rayners Lane to live with Flo's daughter, Nora. Dick died soon after. If Dick did indeed still have the letters, Flo would have found them.

*

According to Nora, Flo destroyed a lot of papers before she died, sitting up late, burning things in the grate.

What was Flo disposing of so assiduously? Did she consider the letters too potentially disturbing? Might they have been amongst the papers that went up in flames?

Nora also reported that Thea visited near the end of Flo's life and that Flo gave Thea a photograph that she wouldn't show to anyone. Evidently, the photo gave Thea a shock – she almost threw it in the fire, then stuffed it into its envelope and ran from the room with tears in her eyes.

Later, she told Nora that the picture was of her grandmother. She described her as a person of no importance in her life. It struck Nora as odd that this 'person of no importance' made Thea so agitated and tearful.

Maybe this was how the picture of Thea's grandmother, Henrietta, came to be hidden in the back of an album, to be discovered some fifty years later by Thea's own granddaughter.

Acknowledgements

Leandra King, founder of English with Leandra, for help with Bajan dialect and idioms.

Lightning Source UK Ltd.
Milton Keynes UK
UKOW04f0805081117
312365UK00001B/146/P